DISTANT RUMBLINGS

LORDS OF ARCADIA
BOOK ONE

JOHN GOODE

Harmony Ink

Published by
Harmony Ink Press
382 NE 191st Street #88329
Miami, FL 33179-3899, USA
publisher@harmonyinkpress.com

Distant Rumblings
Copyright © 2012 by John Goode

Cover Art by Anne Cain   annecain.art@gmail.com
Cover Design by Mara McKennen

ISBN: 978-1-61372-440-8

Printed in the United States of America
First Edition
March 2012

eBook edition available
eBook ISBN: 978-1-61372-441-5

I was always taught that the difference between a dedication and acknowledgement was the difference between standing at home plate and pointing to where you are going to hit and saying "This is for the Gipper," or "The Boys fighting overseas," or even "For Jell-O pudding." Acknowledgements are for the people who taught you how to hit a home run.

With that in mind:

I'd like to dedicate this to the people who made it seem almost easy. To Gayle, who could take a chimp and make the words make sense and is a better writer than she thinks she is. To Gina, who never once sighed when I asked "So that makes sense right?" for the fifteenth time. To Crystal, who should have been writing this with me. To Jason, who honestly did nothing to help in this book except remind me when I needed it that he is my brother. So he did more than he thinks he did.

Now to acknowledge how I got here. To Pam Brekas, my high school journalism teacher who didn't say my stuff sucked. Huge moment for me. To Andy, who understood how important a book like this is to me. To Sue, who without her none of this happens. To Neil Gaiman, for making it look easy. To Douglas Adams, for making it look fun. To John Byrne, who makes it look better than anyone else does. And to my family. Some are gone; some are here. But to quote a great hero of mine: "This is my family. I found it all on my own. It's little, and broken, but still good. Ya. Still good."

But honestly, all of it is because of Eddie, who showed me where the wild stories roam free and graze. Without him, there is no me.

CHAPTER
ONE

I REMEMBER the first time I saw him.

I was walking out of the English hall, and he passed me coming in the door. I had been so busy trying to find a way to hide my useless umbrella that I almost missed him. My father had been going on about a storm that was supposed to hit us for days now, and to be honest, it was getting old. Every day I had brought this idiotic device with me, and each time, I was the only person with an umbrella on a perfectly fine day. This morning, we had actually argued over it, making me miss my bus and therefore miss Jewel, my best friend, altogether. I was trying to find a place under my arm or behind my books and happened to look up as he walked by. I was so shocked, I slammed full force into the guy in front of me. That was the most obviously gay thing I had done so far in high school, and that included my ABBA phase. In my defense, he was the hottest guy I had ever seen in person. To be honest, he was even better looking than the guys I'd seen on TV or in the movies, but that wasn't something I realized at first. All I knew was that a demigod was wandering the halls of Peter Quince High School, and I didn't know who he was.

He passed by me without so much as a sideways glance. In fact, he passed by everybody with the same attitude. On other people, it might have come across as stuck up, but this guy, he seemed almost aloof. It was as if he had no idea how insanely good-looking he was and, because of it, became infinitely more attractive. He had shaggy black hair and blue eyes; he looked about six feet tall and was well proportioned for his size. I apologized to the guy I had plowed into and tried to make sure I had picked up everything I had lost in the exchange. That included my books, umbrella, and dignity all at the same time. Realizing I was going to have to leave one behind, I discarded my dignity and turned to follow him.

I know that sounds completely stalkerish, but let me explain.

My name is Kane Vess, and I have lived in Athens, Iowa, my entire life.

Athens, Iowa, is a small hippie town in the middle of nowhere. Athens, Iowa, is also the weirdest place in the entire world, hands down. My parents moved here when my mom was still pregnant with me, and I have been stuck here ever since. Athens isn't a huge place, so it's not hard to know everyone, if not by name, then at least by face. From time to time, the odd tourist wanders through, but no one ever seems to stay.

I can't say I blame them at all.

The fact that I didn't know tall, dark, and insanely hot was more than a little odd. He didn't look like the rest of the people my age, who were the loud and expressive brood of creative people who believed that labels are toxic and every child is a unique little snowflake. That translated to no dress code, a lot of long hair, and questionable body odor from time to time. It drove me crazy sometimes because it was impossible to stand out in a town full of freaks. I know I'm not supposed to use the word freaks, but I assure you, I've seen TV, and I know the truth. We may think we are the tiny, little center of the world and have the secret of what makes life great, but in fact, we are just another odd, little town in the middle of nowhere, populated by freaks. I was the only openly gay student in town, and the most reaction I ever got was a raised eyebrow by people wondering if I was trying hard enough to be different from everyone else.

The few normal looking people in town—yes, there are a few of us—are not shunned but, more sadly, tolerated by the rest of them. No one ever mocks or picks on people in Athens, but there is a definite cookie given to those who are the most different. People who just get up, dress normal, and do their things are considered people not living up to their life potential, whatever that means. The more adjectives you possessed, the better. For example, Mr. Podduff, who owns Donde está Da Bean, the local coffee shop, is a vegetarian/Taoist/Tantric/Indigo Child healer. I am not sure what all that means, but he does serve a mean latte. If I had ended up being straight, I would have been even more invisible than I already was. It didn't matter anyway; I could have been a Cuban drag queen who wears fruit on his head, and I'd still be nowhere close to my dad's weirdness.

My dad is a flautist. No, that is not what it sounds like. Instead of performing with musical farts, he is a guy who plays a flute. You wouldn't think that would make a person weird, but my dad would shake you of that belief in seconds. He is a folk flutist. Because just playing a flute in general isn't bad enough, he has to play only a special type of flute music that even fewer people listen to. He met my mother in San Francisco, she said he was the best musician in the nine worlds, and they fell in love. Less than a month later they were married and moved to Athens. Why, no one can tell me, but here we moved. My mom died in childbirth, and I have been raised by my dad ever since. Why he stayed here I will never understand, but nothing save zombie attack or an invasion by Republicans will ever get him to leave.

Which means I have been stuck here for sixteen years of bizarreness.

He knew my mother less than a year, but my dad has never stopped loving her. He met the love of his life and treasured every second he had spent with her. He always said she gave me to him, and that was enough. I'd love to work up the sarcasm to think it was totally lame, as all good apathetic teenagers should, but the truth is, I found it completely sweet.

I'd kill for a love like that.

The only gay people I know in town are an older lesbian couple who own Mr. Watson's, the vegan diner on the corner, and Mr. Adler and his lover who own You Must Remember This, the antique store on Fourth Street. By the way, no one uses a normal store name in Athens. I think there's an insane contest to come up with the cutest store name in history whenever a store is scheduled to open. It really is bizarre.

Everyone knows I'm gay, and no one cares, which is good and bad. I mean, I don't want some homophobe jerk to throw a slushie in my face, but to be utterly alone in a town, not because people disapprove of me but simply because the numbers aren't there, sucks.

So trust me, I know it makes me sound like a total creep following this random guy down the hall, but I was desperate to the point that was in no way attractive. I was impressed by the way he maneuvered effortlessly among people; no one seemed to notice him as he dodged between the people walking and texting. Passing by unnoticed couldn't be easy for someone that good-looking; then again, we lived in bizzarro town and were taught from an early age that the cover is the least important part of a book.

But I don't think anyone had seen a book this hot before.

On closer inspection, he was actually about five foot ten but looked taller because of the way he carried himself. It was as if he didn't know how to slouch, his posture was so perfect. His raven black hair was just a bit on the shaggy side but still looked styled. His bangs hung in his eyes, framing his face, which was a true work of art. His features were slender and delicate but in no way conveyed a lack of masculinity. With his solidly defined cheekbones and skinny nose, he would have been too pretty for a guy, but the intensity about him balanced things just enough to make him handsome instead. His worn leather jacket was cut in a style that I'd never seen before. Wearing leather was a big risk in Hippieville, USA, since killing animals for their hides was cruelty, but again, no one even gave him a first glance, much less a second. He wore some kind of canvas backpack slung over his shoulder. At first glance I'd assumed it was from a military surplus store, but as I edged closer to him I could see it was handmade.

There was less than a minute before the next period, and people were now rushing down the hall before they were late. Someone's shoulder hit me from the side, spinning me around for a second. I hadn't been looking where I was going, and it had cost me valuable time. By the time I looked for him again, he was gone. A trick I had no idea how he pulled off. He had to have stepped into one of the classrooms, but I had no idea which one. I was pondering checking them to see which one he was in when the bell rang. I cursed and ran towards my next class. Whoever he was, finding him would have to wait. Besides, it's a small school. I'd see him again.

Lunch came and went, and I didn't see him again.

There weren't enough kids in our school for us to have more than one lunch period. And even if there had been enough, multiple lunch periods just wouldn't have happened. Our parents would have complained about dividing us into arbitrary lunch periods and how one would be favored over the other, and that was fascism, man. Then there would have been an argument about what people had against fascism, since it is just another school of thought, and weren't they just being judgmental? Which would have sparked a debate over whether they were evolving into their parents and if that was a bad thing?

In the meantime, we'd have starved to death.

So every day we all had one big happy lunch outside where we could commune with our true mother (the planet, if you don't speak hippie) and recharge our mana or something. Some of us ate with friends; others meditated. A couple of guys who were the closest thing we had to jocks played Hacky Sack on the lawn as the rest of us tried to enjoy the perfect weather despite my father's warnings of doom.

But no hot guy.

"Your aura is out of sync," Jewel said as I studied the courtyard.

I looked over at her and scowled. "Stop it."

She laughed and rolled her eyes. "You are so easy," she said as she took another bite of her sandwich. "Umbrella again?" she asked as I nodded back. She knew me too well, since we had known each other since we were able to walk. A fellow protestor of our town's new-age sensibility, Jewel Firebird Smith was my partner in crime. I always teased her that her parents had taken such protest in their last name being a bastion of normalcy that they had bestowed her not one but two freakish names in hopes she would escape the gravitational pull of expectations that a name like Smith carried to the rest of the world. She always countered that my last name sounded like something a vampire would say if it was haggling for a better price. "Vess! Vess!" she'd cry out with a lisp until I was crying in laughter.

We never passed up a chance to take a shot at the absurdity of Athens lifestyle. "Are you on the lam or something?" she asked as I continued to scan the crowd. "You look like you're in witness relocation and the bad guys are after you."

"I saw a hot guy today," I said, not even looking back at her.

"Online?" I shook my head. "Here?" she asked, almost choking in disbelief. "In town?"

"In the school," I clarified, which was even harder for her to believe.

"Adam Levine hot or Mark McGrath hot?" she asked.

I sighed. "Not everything in the world is defined by music, you know."

"To you, maybe," she muttered under her breath. Jewel's entire world was defined by music to some degree or another. People were either Jim Morrison cool or Lenny Kravitz hip. They were Beatles classy or Rolling Stones smart. It was like being best friends with an iPod some days, but at least it was her only weird trait.

"A new guy?" she pondered aloud. "That's hard to believe. It'd be all over school by now." She was talking more to herself than me, but she was right.

A new arrival in our little world was usually heralded by some teacher or another making the poor sap stand up and "express himself to the class." The twenty people in that class then went off and shared with the rest of the collective and so on and so on. I joked we didn't need Twitter or Facebook in Athens. Plain old-fashioned gossip moved much faster.

"And yet I saw him," I said, sounding surer than I felt. At this point in the day, word of a new student should have been all over school; whether talking about looks was superficial or not, no one that handsome could be missed for long.

"So how cute?" she asked, leaning forward in anticipation. She wasn't the prettiest girl in the world, but I thought she was adorable. She believed herself too big to be attractive to others, but I thought that was an excuse for her to not even try.

I looked backed and admitted, "Darren Criss hot."

She gasped, there being no higher compliment I could give anyone.

We tossed our trash into the proper recycling bin before we made our way back to class. Had I become so desperate that I was imagining guys now? How sad was that? Bad enough that I was in a state of perpetual solitary confinement, but having to wait until I went to college was driving me nuts. I mean, was I just a few bad days away from thinking I was Brad Pitt in disco glasses blowing buildings up? I wasn't sure what was worse, going crazy or the fact that he wasn't real.

"You coming over after school?" she asked as we began to part ways.

"Do I ever not come over?" I asked.

"Ouch. Someone is testy," she said in mock pain.

"I'm sorry, I just...," I began to explain.

"I'm kidding!" she said, blowing me an air kiss as the bell rang. "Later, gator."

As I dragged my way to class, I tried not to look like I'd just had to put my dog down. I tried, but I'm pretty sure I failed kind of hard.

The rest of the day seemed dimmer than normal. I wandered through elective science, which was Athens-speak for a class describing one way the physical universe could be explained, but, hey, no pressure, man. After that was drama with Ms. Brody, a plus-sized woman who may have once wandered onstage in a theater just a few blocks away from Broadway, which made her an "actress," a word she always said with a small hand flourish and a half bow to an imaginary crowd.

She went on and on about our spring production and how incredible it was going to be, but I wasn't listening anymore.

I couldn't shake the image of my mystery boy. Had I made him up? It wasn't outside the realm of possibility that it was someone else that I had seen at an odd angle and thought was someone new. But there wasn't anyone in school close to as good-looking as this guy had been. Hippie town or not, there were a few genetically gifted guys that no unflattering poncho or unsightly Birkenstocks could diminish. But I knew them all and also knew that not one of them could have made my head turn like this guy had. Then again, I had grown up with everyone in this school, so it would have felt like being attracted to your brother or something if he was one of them.

"And you, Mr. Vess?"

I looked up, stunned, as I realized the entire room was staring at me.

I bit the inside of my cheek as I realized I had zoned out so much that I had stopped paying attention to her presentation. Not having any idea what she might have been talking about, I answered, "Um, present?"

There was muffled laughter from people covering their mouths, and I knew that was the wrong answer.

"Well perhaps right now, but you have been sorely lacking for the last"—she looked at her watch—"seventeen minutes, so maybe you can explain to us the plot of *A Midsummer Night's Dream* by the great William Shakespeare?"

I could not. In fact, with a gun to my head, I couldn't have picked Shakespeare out of a lineup with three boring playwrights and a crib sheet. Knowing there was no way she was going to let me go until I gave an answer of some kind, I took a deep breath and offered up, "A dream, that um, was in the summer?" I saw the shocked looks on the other kids' faces and added, "At night?"

You could swear I had insulted Liza Minnelli and *Rent* at the same time. I hated that people thought just because I was gay I would be into drama. It was an ugly stereotype that just was not true since I loathed being on stage more than anything in the world. I volunteered for anything backstage each time we had a production, against the strong objections of Ms. Brody, who said I was a butterfly just waiting to come out of his cocoon.

A butterfly? Really?

"No, but thank you for trying," she said, pacing the stage like she owned it. "The play is actually two stories intertwined together that come from two completely different places. The first one is about a girl who is forced to choose between marrying a man she doesn't love or becoming a nun while the second one is about the king and queen of fairies who are having an argument over the fate of a child who is a shape shifter. The king sends his henchman, Puck, to ensorcel his wife so she may forget the child. What happens next is a wild adventure that is just—" She clapped her hands in excitement. "Oh, you will just love it!"

A couple of kids shared in her exuberance as I tried not to shake my head in disbelief.

"One of the things I want to explore in this production is the motivation of Puck throughout the play. He is a trickster and loves chaos, but what is it he is truly after?"

One of the kids called out, "Sex!" Which brought laughter to the rest of us.

"Well, not sex as much as passion...," she began to correct him.

"Hot mothers!" another screamed.

"And Quinn!"

She tried to wave her hands to get us under control, but she was painfully *Glee* ignorant and had lost control of the class.

The day couldn't end fast enough for me.

I practically sprinted to my locker to ditch my books before I met Jewel out front. If anyone could make me forget what had happened, it would be her and one of her truly awful independent bands. Screeching vocals with barely tolerable instrumentals would be the only thing that could banish the image of my imaginary boy from my mind and hopefully give me some peace.

And then he walked right by me.

My head spun so fast I swear I got dizzy. I dropped the book in my hand as I watched him examine the lockers carefully, obviously reading the numbers posted on the top of each one. He kept glancing to a small slip of paper and back to the locker as I held my breath in fear he might suddenly vanish. Never taking my eyes off of him, I knelt down and grabbed my book and shoved it back in the locker, pushing aside the useless umbrella to make room. I slowly closed my locker, trying to make as little noise as possible, as if I was watching a deer drink from a stream instead of a guy opening his locker. His face was obscured as he opened the door and removed the pack from his shoulder.

I tried to be as quiet as one can be in sneakers on a tile floor as I approached him before he could vanish again. I had no idea what I was going to say, but making sure he was flesh and blood was a good start. Maybe I'd welcome him to the school and the town. Though I wished he was gay, even if he was straight, the chance to slowly ease someone into the chaos that was Athens would increase the chance of normalcy around here by at least a small percentage.

He was wearing boots that looked similar in construction to his jacket. By that I meant they looked handmade instead of store bought. In Athens, more than a few people made their own clothes and clothes for others. All natural, homespun cloth with wooden buttons guaranteed to make even stylish people look like Amish rejects, it was a rarity to find actual fashionable clothes to wear within fifty miles. Another clue he wasn't from around here. Mystery Boy's jacket was sweet. It was a shade of smooth, brown leather that I had to ask how was achieved. I couldn't guess the animal the brown leather had come from, but I wanted to touch it to see if it was as smooth as it seemed. The boots were a little too worn for my taste, but they accented his ruggedness, minimizing his innate prettiness.

I was within two steps of him when I decided to reach out and knock on his locker door. My knuckles were less than a quarter inch away when he slammed the door shut violently. I froze as he lunged at me. A blur of motion, a glint of metal in his hand. Then he slammed the metal into my chest.

I looked down in shock. The hilt of a sword stuck out where I was always told my heart was located. His face was next to mine as he hissed, "Die, assassin."

I swear nothing in this town was ever normal.

(HAPTER TWO

I SAW my fifth birthday party; bubbles danced around my backyard as my father played his flute. I saw Jeanie Francis kiss me when I was eight, the thought I was sure I had just been infected with a terminal case of cooties filling my mind. I saw myself at eleven having a sleep over with Leon Parsky, wondering why I wanted to kiss him a thousand times more than I had ever wanted to kiss Jeanie Francis. I saw myself at fourteen sitting across from my dad, squirming as he explained that there was nothing wrong with liking boys, and he was more than willing to accept me and my lifestyle.

It was my entire, miserable life passing before my eyes, and I realized how incredibly lame it was.

A second passed, and I waited for the pain to start. I'd just been stabbed by a crazed fashion model in the hall of my high school, and I had no reaction? Nothing in my life had prepared me for something like this to happen. I hated that even as he glared at me, waiting for my pierced heart to stop beating, that he looked even better than I had first thought. I could see a ring of lighter blue around his pupil, and I casually thought that must be why his eyes seemed to twinkle so much. Another second passed, and neither of us moved as we both waited for something to happen that obviously wasn't. Another second passed, and I realized I was confused but not in pain. I stared down at the hilt, and I saw him do the same half a second later. He had it gripped with both hands, and the base of it was pressed firmly against my chest, yet there was no blood or pain.

I looked back up at him, and our eyes met.

The anger in his face melted into confusion and then undeniable chagrin. He slowly stepped back, and I watched the blade slide out from my chest in amazement. I had begun to think that it was one of those collapsible blades magicians use, but it was obviously real metal that he was pulling out of me painlessly. In that panicked moment, I estimated it to be more than twelve inches long, and the metal it was made from had a blue hue to it. I'd never seen that before in the weapons that were made around town by Renaissance Fair fanatics. It was engraved completely in runes, which made it look more like something out of *Lord of the Rings* than an actual weapon. Once he pulled it free, the metal changed color from blue back to a normal silver; I stood in front of him, blinking.

"You're not a Dark," he whispered. The emphasis on the "dark" meant it was a name instead of just the word. Already paler than most people, his skin seemed almost paper white. His hands moved so fast they blurred as he tossed the blade into his pack and closed it quickly. "Apologies," he mumbled as he stepped away, obviously trying to flee the scene.

That was when my brain started working again.

"Hey!" I called out, grabbing his shoulder. "What the hell was that?"

His entire body moved back toward me as his shoulder ducked under my grip, and he faced me. I could see the crystal blue of his eyes and could see the light blue were like particles of ice now as he seemed to stare through me, past my face, into my mind. "Forget this happened," he commanded in a tone that sounded like he was used to being obeyed.

We stood there for a few seconds before I exclaimed, "You have to be kidding me! You just stabbed me!"

The baffled look on his face would have been endearing if he hadn't recently buried a knife in me. He reached out and grabbed my shoulders. I wondered for a second if he was going to kiss me and then he repeated with more force, "You will forget this happened!"

"I really won't," I stated flatly, wondering why all the hot ones were crazy.

He stumbled back a few steps. For the first time gravity seemed to affect him like the rest of us, and he lurched to the side.

"That's…," he stammered. "That's impossible."

"You *do* know you can't even have a knife at this school," I protested as my shock wore off.

He continued to back away from me as if *I* was the one who had stabbed *him*. Still gaping, he bumped into the door and fumbled it open. "Stay away," he warned warily as he turned and rushed down the steps.

"As if!" I shouted, chasing after him.

I bolted out the doors seconds after him, but he was gone. I searched the front of the school for him but saw no one. He had vanished on me for a second time, and the trick was getting annoying fast. I looked down and touched my shirt where his blade had stabbed me and saw nothing at all. Not a rip or a tear was anywhere to be found. I pulled it back and looked down at my chest, and it was equally unmarked.

"How the hell did he do that?" I asked myself.

"There's fashionably late and there's you," Jewel called across the lawn toward me. "Come on!" She gestured at me to move, and I had to admit, he was nowhere to be seen. There wasn't much sense in scouring the school for someone who was clearly not there anymore. Shaking my head, I ran over to her, vowing that whatever was going on with this boy was far from over.

FROM the shadows cast by the shrubbery he peered out at the strange boy who had not been affected by Truheart and wondered again how he had resisted his Charms. "He isn't one of the Dark," he said out loud.

"We can't be sure," a disembodied voice snapped grumpily.

"He wasn't affected by the blade, trust me. That is not an agent of the Dark," the boy insisted.

"I should end him," the voice added.

"No," he said quickly. "If he isn't affected by my blade he must be pure of heart." He watched the boy leave with the strange girl and added, "I'll look into it. Leave it to me."

The other voice grumbled, "I say we should kill him."

He chuckled and shook his head. "You say that about everyone."

"And I'm always right," the voice countered.

He couldn't argue with the voice's sentiment. However, the boy intrigued him; there would be time to kill him later, if necessary.

"OKAY, that's the third horrible song in a row, and you haven't complained once."

I looked up and saw Jewel staring at me from her bed.

"Sorry," I said, sighing to myself and lying back on the floor. "Bad day."

Or good day since I wasn't dead and bleeding in the hallway in front of my locker.

"It's not like you won't find a guy, you know," she said, rolling onto her back, looking at the plastic stars on her ceiling. "Once you get pardoned to college, that is."

Normally, one of our favorite hobbies involved sitting in Jewel's or my room and idly speculating about what we'd do once we left Athens. She was convinced she was going to be a band manager or band promoter or band groupie. She wasn't sure which, but she was going to have to do something with a band. My plans changed by the minute, but I knew if I was flipping burgers and sleeping on a couch in an apartment I shared with four people, life would be better than being stuck in this tar pit of a town.

"I'm gonna go," I said, slipping my shoes back on and grabbing my bag.

"We can listen to some of your crappy music if things are that bad," Jewel offered in an attempt to console me, even though she had no idea why I was acting like an idiot. "Look, I have Backstreet Boys!"

"It's not the music," I said quickly. "It's just...." Glumly, I realized I couldn't explain how Athens had just scored eleven out of ten on the weirdness scale. "...I'll see you tomorrow," I finished, and left as fast as I could.

I felt bad about just bailing on her, but I knew she'd just chalk everything up to me being a drama junkie and forgive me tomorrow.

I bundled up my coat as I realized it was getting slightly colder.

I'd never thought about dying before today but realizing that someone just stabbed you in the heart has a way of bringing those thoughts to the forefront something fierce. If I had died, the most miserable excuse for a life ever would have ended. At the very worst, my dad would be sad, Jewel would have an excuse to wear a lot of black, and the forty-three Facebook friends I had would wonder why all my crops were dead and why I never posted anymore.

My life was just so pathetic I felt like crying.

I made my way directly home, not even pausing to get something to eat for me and my dad from Mr. Watson's like I normally did. I just needed to be in motion for some reason. If I was avoiding traffic while crossing a street and ignoring people, I wouldn't have time to think about how useless my life had been up to this point.

HE FOLLOWED the boy from a safe distance.

If the stranger had any training in espionage he certainly didn't show it as he made his way across the town. The sun was setting, and there were more than enough shadows for him to conceal himself in case the boy turned around.

So far, he was not overly impressed with this world. The people were ugly, dim, and showed no aptitude for The Arts. Servant stock at best, they seemed to have no ruling class, which was distressing on many counts. He wasn't sure what was the dominant class here, and he wasn't sure he wanted to.

His prey was passable to his eyes, though. He wasn't a noble. The boy would have been acceptable as a pleasurling in the right light. He was more concerned about how the human had resisted not only his blade but his Charms. Though seemingly in decent shape, he gave no indication of formal Training. To be honest, there was doubt that this side even had such schools to begin with since magic here was almost nonexistent. Centuries had passed on his side, which meant almost a millennium here since his people had walked this world. He highly doubted that any of his kind had survived for so long unaided, much less thrived enough to pass on their skills.

The boy entered what the humans called a "house." He considered it barely a hovel, but when in Arcadia....

"Rome," he muttered under his breath, remembering the lesson he had learned in the human academy today. "It's Rome on this side." He chastised himself for his ignorance as he crossed the street into the boy's yard. He bounded up the tree as if half cat and perched on a limb, concealed from all sight. Shivering a bit, he tightened his coat around him and waited.

I TOSSED my bag into the corner as I kicked off my shoes.

"Dad, I'm home!" I yelled, knowing he was most likely back in his studio, out of hearing. When there was no reply, I nodded and made my way to the kitchen. I poured myself some apple juice as I began to thumb through our collection of take-out menus. I knew rationally that there was no other place that offered food like we ate here in Athens, but I had never known any other cuisine. Where normal people chose between Chinese and pizza, I was deciding between Tofu Togo and Wizard of Wok.

"Kane? Are you home?" my dad called, coming down the stairs.

"In here!" I called back as I decided on Wizard. "I'm ordering from the Wok, what do you want?"

He came around the corner. "You didn't bring anything?" he asked, clearly disappointed.

"Yeah, spaced it out," I lied and grabbed the phone off the wall. "What do you want?"

"Fourteen with extra onions," he replied as he opened the fridge in hopes food might have magically appeared. He sighed heavily when he realized it hadn't.

"Hi, I'd like to place an order for delivery," I said and then read off the menu.

HE WATCHED through the window as the boy used the "tellyphone" as Spike had called it. It was some kind of communication device, and he wasn't entirely convinced it wasn't some kind of Sending. He could see the boy's lips move, but the shapes his mouth made were gibberish to him. The bauble allowed him to understand their language, but from his vantage point, with a closed window between him and the conversation, it was useless.

The father seemed as unappealing as everyone else. He was powerfully unattractive with a head of long gray hair and a pair of thick spectacles. Whatever remarkable traits the boy possessed, they hadn't come from his father.

They continued to talk between themselves, which was more aggravating than watching nothing at all. He needed to know more, and sitting out in the Dark on a tree branch was not going to achieve it. He began to climb higher up the tree and then stepped out onto the branch that had grown toward the house. The branches that far up were so slender that they shouldn't have been able to support his weight, yet the skeleton-like twig fingers didn't budge as he edged closer and closer toward the house. There was a foul chill in the air that promised a storm eventually, and Hawk didn't like it at all.

Silently, he judged his distance and jumped across the gap, landing and clinging to the side of the house like a piece of metal to a magnet. The nearest window was locked, but he could see the mechanism from where he clung. He rapped on the window twice, whispering a word that the wind dispelled as he spoke it.

Seconds later, he pulled open the window and made his way inside, closing it behind him silently. He paused for a moment, listening, and the two people's voices drifted upward into the range of the bauble. He smiled as their gibberish became understandable.

"SO HOW was your day?" my dad asked after I hung up.

For some reason, telling him I got stabbed in the chest and didn't die seemed like a bad idea, so instead I gave my usual "It was cool."

"Any homework?" I shook my head no. "Any rain?" he inquired, which was him going for the Dad of the Year award compared to his normal level of interest in school.

I looked over at him with a "give me a break" look. "What's up?" I asked him.

He sighed and sat down, looking more like a kid who got caught in a lie than a father. "My agent called today."

"You still have an agent?" I probably shouldn't have sounded that surprised.

"You do know I make music for a living right?" he responded with just a little more sarcasm than was needed.

"I didn't know you needed an agent to play a flute."

"Without that flute...," he began. Helpfully, I finished the sentence for him. "...I wouldn't be alive. I know, I know."

"Anyway," he pressed on, ignoring my usual apathy for all aspects of his career. "She called and said there is a gig starting this weekend and could extend till next week."

"A paying gig?" I still could not believe someone would pay to hear what I put my iPod on to escape.

His eyes narrowed in annoyance. "Yes. It's in Berkeley, and they are only willing to pay for me."

I wasn't sure who else they were supposed to pay for when I

realized what Dad meant.

"You mean me?" I asked, pointing at myself. "Why would I want to go?"

"It's a festival. They want me for five days, and I don't feel right leaving you alone for that long," he lamented, meaning he had already turned the gig down.

"Dad," I said, trying hard not to roll my eyes. "I am almost seventeen years old. You do know I can stay by myself and not go all *Lord of the Flies* right?"

He stared at me for a long second. "I was more thinking *Home Alone.*"

Now I did roll my eyes. "Dad, come on!"

"Five days is a long time, Kane," he tried to reason with me.

"No it isn't. Look, Jewel's mom can check up on me, and you can call every day," I argued. "You haven't played live since—" And I stopped myself. "—for a long time," I amended. "You should do this."

"What if it rains?"

"*Dad!*"

He seemed skeptical, but I could tell he really wanted to go. "And you wouldn't be mad?" he asked sheepishly.

"Mad? Why would I be mad?"

In a small voice he explained, "I haven't left you alone that long, ever."

"Look, Dad, you raised me, and by the way, bravo on that." That made him smile. "You put your life on hold long enough. If you want to go, then go. Seriously, I am in no way going to be mad."

"Really?" he asked hopefully.

"For reals," I assured him. "'Sides I could do with you not being underfoot all the time."

He laughed. "You sound like your mother."

Which was about the greatest compliment he could give another person.

"I'll go call Jenny and tell her I can go," he said excitedly. He seemed years younger as he turned and bounded up the stairs.

"Kids," I said out loud, chuckling.

THE father walked right past him as he climbed the stairs, never noticing.

He resisted the urge to let out a sigh of relief; after all, his Charms could only mask so much. He still had no idea how the boy had seen him at the academy, but whatever skill the son had, it was not passed down from the father. Hawk carefully made his way down the stairs, making sure he kept himself light in case they had a tendency to creak.

The place was filthy, at least by his standards. If his mother had ever seen their domicile in such a state, she would have executed the entire staff as a cautionary lesson to others. The boy's house was miserably small, though. Perhaps they had no cleaning people.

The thought alone made him shiver.

He edged down the last few steps and took a careful look around the corner. The boy sat at a small rectangle-shaped table and placed something into his ears. He had seen other youths with similar appliances dangling from their ears earlier and assumed they were some form of protection. From what, he had no idea. He didn't think humans suffered from any vulnerability from Music like his own people did. In fact, this place seemed devoid of anything that he would consider a predator, unless he counted the filth. The entire town could be considered one step above a dumping ground in Arcadia and that was only because of its lack of visible corpses. Spike had advised him repeatedly to learn tolerance; he had reminded Spike to remember his place.

"I got it!" the father exclaimed as he rushed down the stairs. The stranger pressed himself up against the wall as the man passed by him, unaware how close he had been to colliding with him. "She said I got it!"

The boy didn't respond; curious, he looked around the corner to see the interaction. The father waved his hand in front of boy's face. "Hey!" he called out. Startled, the boy looked up and pulled out the stoppers. He could hear the very distant strains of what he had already discovered this side called "just music" coming from them. A Music device? Or perhaps a device to cancel out Music? That would be ingenious. The older man repeated, "I got it! I leave tomorrow!"

"Awesome, Dad," the boy replied.

He wasn't sure what an awesome was, but he believed it was a form of adulation for them.

"Okay I need to collect my stuff. Can you call Jewel's parents so I can talk to them?" The man spoke quickly as he turned back toward the stairs. "Let me know when the food arrives!" he added as he climbed the steps by two and three at a time.

Hawk stood there, trying to decipher the meaning of their conversation, when he saw the boy look up and look directly at him.

MY DAD was such a spaz I had to love it.

He sounded shocked that the lady who had called him and asked him to play would then say she wanted him to come and play. I may not like his music, but I do know he is very good.

And the boy from school was standing at the foot of my stairs peeking into the kitchen.

"*Hey!*" I shouted, lunging to my feet and sending my chair flying.

I saw the same look of shock and outrage on his face when he realized I had seen him. Startled, he ducked back around the corner toward the stairs. I ran the few feet from the table to the door, expecting to see him escaping up them, but the stairway was empty. Which, once again, should have been impossible.

I bolted up as fast as I could and saw the door to my room swinging shut.

With no idea what I was going to do if I caught him, I charged after him, throwing my door open with a loud, "A ha!"

But my room was empty. I saw my curtains blowing freely from the open window. I felt the night air as I walked cautiously to the window and then looked down across our very empty yard. A dog barked out in the distance. No one could have made it up those stairs and out a second-story window that quickly, it was humanly impossible.

The doorbell rang, breaking my concentration.

"What in the hell?" I muttered, closing my window and locking it. The delivery guy rang the bell again as I turned and ran down the stairs. "*Hold on!*" I screamed in frustration.

THIS time he did let out a sigh of relief as he clung to the roof, mere inches away from the top of the boy's window. Twice the boy had seen him, and this time he had been consciously using his Charm to mask his presence.

There was no way the boy was a Dark, and he seemed to possess no Arts to speak of, yet he was immune to every one of Hawk's abilities.

"I hate this world," he muttered to himself as he flipped down to the windowsill and then back to the tree. Within seconds he was gone, wondering what exactly was going on and deciding to think about it when he had more time.

CHAPTER THREE

A DAY that had started out as weird and progressed to bizarre had now evolved to almost terrifying, and I wasn't sure how to handle it.

My dad was so jazzed about his trip that he didn't even notice me walking around the house checking every window and door to make sure they were locked. I wanted to tell my dad not to go, but what could he do if he stayed in Athens? I saw no evidence other than my open window. Without using a ladder or wings I wasn't sure how he could have gotten that far up. I was sure Dad had passed the guy on the stairs and hadn't seen him, which either meant he had been invisible or I was imagining him. I honestly didn't know which possibility was worse.

I have no idea how I got to sleep, but at some point, I did.

When my alarm clock went off for school, I woke up almost screaming, picturing someone sneaking into my room with a blue-bladed knife. I was completely exhausted and wide-awake at the same time, and it sucked. When I got downstairs and saw my dad dressed in his best jeans with suitcases by the door, I was confused, until I remembered he was really leaving.

I felt cold terror seize my heart, but I refused to let it show on my face. I wasn't going to be a baby and start crying just because my dad was leaving and A&F models were sneaking around my house. I would figure mystery boy out by myself and not worry him.

That or I'd sleep over at Jewel's every night until my dad came back.

"Okay there's some money on the kitchen table," he said when he saw me walking down the stairs. "I left the hotel number as well as Jenny's in case you can't get me on my cell," he continued, explaining rapidly.

"And if things get bad I can flash a light with a giant flute symbol in it right?" I mocked, knowing if I didn't give him a little sass he'd suspect something was up.

"This is my first time, let me be worried," he tried to reason with me.

"We all knew this day would come, Dad. It was just a matter of time before you grew up and spread your wings." I placed my hand on my heart. "I'll get by, but as long as you are happy that's all that matters."

"You know I am going to say nothing like that when you leave for college," he said, with his hands on his hips.

I raised an eyebrow. "I bet you squirt a tear out before I get to the curb."

He smiled back. "I'll have your room cleared out before you hit the city limits."

A car's horn honked outside.

"That's my cab," he said, turning to the door then back to me. "You're sure you'll be okay?"

I forced myself to remain smiling as I nodded. "Peachy with a side of keen."

He opened his arms, and I moved in to hug him. "Call me if you need anything, okay? And if starts to rain…," he began.

"I will melt as my kind is known to do." I smiled as reassuringly as possible. "I'll be fine, Dad."

He patted my back and then grabbed his bags. "I'll call you when I land."

"Try to have fun," I pleaded as he walked toward the curb.

He tossed his bags in the trunk and stared back at me. "You too."

And then his face got serious. "But not too much fun."

I gave him a fake salute. "Sir, yes, sir."

He stuck his tongue out at me as he got in the backseat of the cab.

It took everything I had not to scream for him to stop and beg him to stay. Instead, I forced myself to watch, waving the entire time, as his cab drove off.

When I turned around and looked at the house, it didn't feel anything like the place where I'd lived my entire life. I looked down at myself and said out loud, "Well, I can't go to school like this." And marched back inside. I tried not to notice how overcast the sky was.

I locked both locks behind me.

"So, WE aren't killing him?" the black cat asked.

He stood shirtless, his skin smooth and toned in the morning light. He only had two adornments on his person, yet each one stood out like a beacon. He had one earring in his left ear, a single green gem that was concealed by his hair, and a golden chain around his neck. Dangling from the chain, between the clefts of his pecs, was an acorn that was seemingly made out of solid gold. A stray beam of sunlight hit its surface, and it seemed to glow iridescent for a moment. He pulled a shirt over his perfectly muscled chest and ran a hand through his hair. "I already said we weren't."

The cat paced the floor of the abandoned house, its tail jerking violently. "That was before he saw through your concealment. He *has* to have been trained."

"Spike, I am telling you, he has no training whatsoever." He pulled on his jacket. "There is something different about him."

The cat's form began to swell and grow, the black coat turning a pale white as more muscle formed around its frame. Within seconds, what had been a black cat became a white and tan bulldog. Spike turned and looked at him. "Different is never good."

Hawk rolled his eyes as he grabbed his pack. "This entire world is different. It's nothing like what the books tell us."

"What ever is?" the dog replied, sitting down. "If we aren't going to kill him, we should move on." The dog's fur began to darken to a pale gray as its snout elongated. Now a silver timber wolf looked at him. "My job is to protect you."

He was checking the contents of the bag as he commented, "You are here to protect me in whatever course I decide to take." His tone grew sterner. "It is best to remember that my course is my choice."

The wolf lay down; as he cowered he shrank back into cat form. "I wasn't challenging your authority," the creature began.

"Of course you weren't," the boy interrupted. "I've said we are staying, and he is not to be killed. I do not wish to go over this again."

The cat bowed slightly. "As you command, Prince Ha—"

"I am not that here!" the boy said harshly, his emotion startling the cat, which recoiled from his tone. Taking a deep breath, he forced his handsome features to relax as he rubbed the bridge of his nose. "Even alone we must strive to maintain our cover. If you are to refer to me by name, refer to me as Hawk. Never my title."

"Yessir," the cat answered meekly. The boy shot the creature a stern look, and he amended with, "Yes, Hawk?"

"Better," he said, nodding. He opened the bag and held it out. "In you go."

The cat took three running steps toward him as its fur began to melt into feathers. By the third step he was no larger than a kitten and had wings. He took flight as its back paws became talons, and a tiny black sparrow dived into the pack. The boy fastened it shut.

"Let me know if you need to get out. I had to throw that book away yesterday."

"Sorry," a voice mumbled from inside the pack.

The boy rolled his eyes and grumbled under his breath, "Changelings."

I WAS jittery as a long-tailed cat in a room full of rocking chairs as I searched the school for him again. I looked everywhere for him, but he was nowhere to be seen. I still couldn't understand how anyone that good-looking could go unseen in such a small school. On second thought, I was talking about the same guy who managed to get into my house via the second-floor window without a ladder; anything was possible.

"Reach for the sky!" a voice said from behind me as something poked me in the back.

My reaction shocked me as much as it shocked Jewel. I spun around, slamming my backpack into her. She went flying back onto her ass, sliding a few feet from the impact. In a normal school, what I'd done would have been met with laughing and pointing. After all, nothing funnier than a big girl falling on her ass. But Athens is so far from normal you couldn't even reach it by text if you needed to. Everyone stared at me like I had grown a second head and began spouting blood. No, scratch that, if that had happened they'd have welcomed me as a new life form and brought me love and joy. They looked at me like I was Richard Nixon. Violence of any kind was forbidden within the halls of Peter Quince High School. Jewel looked up at me with shock in her eyes as I tried to explain what had just happened. "I didn't, I mean, I was...," I stammered as someone helped her up.

"What is wrong with you?" she asked, obviously trying not to cry. That fall had to have hurt.

"I just...," I began to say and then saw the dozens of stares boring holes into my head. This was too much attention for me, the exact reason I stayed off the stage. Knowing there was no excuse other than the fact that I was losing my mind, I turned and fled the scene.

I ducked into the theater, knowing this early it would be empty.

The sound of the doors closing echoed throughout the space as I ran toward the stairs to the stage. There was a half-painted forest on the stage, Ms. Brody getting a head start for the fall production no doubt. Backstage, I pushed past the rack of costumes and knelt down with my back against the wall. I was shaking I was so upset, and I couldn't stop. I was afraid, angry, and confused all at once, and the combination was killing me.

I had to know what was going on, and the only one who could explain was my mysterious boy. Of course I had no idea how to find him and what I'd say even if I did. Twenty-four hours ago I hated my boring life. Now, all I wanted was for it to be boring again.

I didn't want to cry, didn't want to be that little bitch of a person, but the tears came anyway. And as I huddled there, I heard something move out on the stage. I began to stand up as a figure walked toward me; I couldn't tell who it was because of the damn tears. I wiped my eyes, and I saw him walk out of the shadows of the theater.

It was my boy.

"You," he said, pointing at me. "I've been looking for you." His voice was odd, some kind of an accent I couldn't place. Half Australian, half European, it was like nothing I'd heard before. I knew I should have been scared, but for some reason, I didn't sense anything hostile from him at all.

"You're real," I said more than asked, marveling that he was actually real.

He cocked his head, confused, and it made all the harshness vanish from his face for a second. He was incredible. I could see now he was in better shape than I had noticed before, he filled the jacket out perfectly, confirming that it had to have been made just for him. His jeans were well worn but it looked from actual age rather than style. They looked ancient but well cared for, which just added more questions than answers.

"I don't understand. Of course I'm real," he said hesitantly. "Do you have dreamlings here?"

"Have what?" I asked, the certainty I had that he was real fading again.

"Dreamlings," he said again. "Wandering nightmares?" He gestured with his hands. "Walking dreams?" I shook my head silently. "It's unimportant," he said, dismissing it. "You saw me yesterday." Not a question but a fact. I nodded all the same. "How?"

Again, I understood the words but not the question. He seemed frustrated, but I felt no real anger. There was a difference between an unknown wandering my house and this very real person standing in front of me. I considered his question and then opted for the truth. "My eyes?"

His eyes narrowed in frustration. "I don't have time for your insolence, boy!"

It was the "boy" that struck me a like a slap across the face.

"Excuse me?" I said, finding my voice. "You stabbed me in the heart yesterday, so I'll be as insolent as I want to be, thank you! By the way, you don't look a day older than me! Don't call me *boy* again," I threatened.

He stood up straighter and glared, looking like something out of Method Acting 101 Affronted Indignation by Ms. Brody. "I will not be addressed like that."

I took a step toward him. "Look, you may think you're hot shit, but trust me, you don't impress me." It was a lie, but there was no way I was going to admit he was exactly my type.

The whole haughty demeanor look faded for a second as he asked, "Why would I think I am heated excrement?" A small pause. "Is that what your kind finds attractive?" he asked with barely disguised disgust on his face.

"My kind?" I demanded. "Is that a crack about being gay?"

More confusion. "You're happy? I don't understand. What does that have to do with anything?"

Now I paused. "What?"

"You said, is that a crack about being happy. I assume crack is a word for statement, but why would being happy matter?" he countered.

"I said *gay*."

He nodded. "Yes, happy."

"*Gay!*" I shouted. "As in, I like other men."

"You like...," he began to say and then stopped. "You mean as in...?" He made a gesture that I didn't understand, but I nodded anyway. A few seconds passed and then he seemed to get it. "Oh, you enjoy males more than women," he said excitedly. "And that is what makes you happy? Why didn't you say so? I find males much more pleasurable as well. Are you trying to initiate sexual activities now?"

"Yes. Wait, no. I mean... hold on," I said, closing my eyes and taking a second for the blush on my face to diminish. "I am saying the word gay."

He nodded. "Happy."

I looked suspiciously at him to make sure he wasn't joking with me. "Yes, *gay* can mean happy, but it means other things too." His face reflected his bewilderment. "You know that, right?"

"Happy means happy?" he asked, his earlier arrogance gone. He reached up and began fumbling with a small-jeweled earring I hadn't seen under his hair. "I think this enchantment is corrupted," he grumbled under his breath.

My first thought was that he was crazy, but in this town, crazy had several different levels, and he was barely scratching the surface, which meant in Athens, he was just eccentric. There was an artist who lived on the outskirts of town who thought she was a vampire. She honestly believed she was an undead, blood-sucking vampire. She only came into town in late afternoon, and she had a cloak and everything. *She* was crazy. This guy just seemed confused, like English wasn't his first language. I stepped closer, eying the jewel.

"Is that a radio?" I asked. "Are you talking to someone?" I reached up to touch it, and he slapped my hand away.

"What in the nine worlds is a radio?" he asked, snapping at me. "By the gods, make sense!"

"Me?" I exploded, rubbing my hand. "Dude, you are the weirdest person I have ever met! Trust me! In this town, that's saying something!"

"What are you?" he asked suddenly.

"Kane," I shot back. "Kane Vess. And you?"

He blinked a few times in confusion before answering. "I am… I am called Hawk."

"Hippie parents too?" I asked with some sympathy. After all, my best friend is named Jewel.

He scrunched his face again. "Hippie?" He sighed, shaking his head. "This is hopeless," he said, sitting down on the stage. "They warned me that colloquialisms and idioms would remain unchanged, but none of your people seem to want to speak proper English at all."

My people? Okay: second level of crazy.

I knelt down. "Let's try this again." I started slowly. "Where are you from?"

He looked up at me, and I felt my heart skip a beat as those eyes looked into mine. "A long way away." And then in a lower voice as he looked back at the stage, "And I'll never get back."

My common sense told me not to trust him. Everything that was rational in my mind screamed at me to walk away while I could. It was obvious he was crazy, I just didn't know how crazy yet. I don't know if it was because he was so incredible looking or because he seemed so sad, but I knew I couldn't just walk away.

"Do you need help, Hawk?" I asked. "Because you seem like you need a friend."

He looked up at me, expressionless but with pleading eyes. "Do I look that pathetic?"

I shook my head. "No. You just look lost." I held out my hand. "Let me help." And then I added, "Please?"

He hesitated for a second, and then, with a smile that made me swoon inside, he reached out and took my hand. I took it back and squeezed it firmly.

And that was the moment my life changed forever.

(HAPTER
FOUR

"SO YOU want to tell me who you are, and what's going on?" I asked, sitting down next to him, knowing I was going to miss first period but somehow not caring at all.

He was hesitant to start, which told me whatever it was he thought it was important. In my experience, I had found that people who answer too quickly are usually lying. He came off so lost, which of course hit all my buttons because who doesn't dream of finding an incredibly hot boy and fixing him? Straight guys may have cars and gadgets, but girls and gay boys, we like to fix broken boys.

And Hawk was so beautifully broken.

I forced myself to remember that this was the same guy who had shoved a knife into my heart not even twelve hours before, but it wouldn't take. However, instead of remembering the cold triumph in his eye as he stabbed me, I just seemed to recall his embarrassment afterward as he apologized. I was praying my instincts were right, and I wasn't just some insecure creep willing to forgive anything a hot guy did because I wanted to kiss him so badly.

"I am not from here," he said, tracing a pattern in the stage floor, not making eye contact. I waited for him to say more, but it was obvious even that much was an effort for him. This was like pulling teeth he was so reluctant. Even getting him to look up was impossible.

"I knew that," I said, trying to encourage him verbally. Now he looked up, those devastatingly blue eyes boring a hole through me.

Obviously, I had said the wrong thing, so I clarified. "I mean, I know everyone in Athens, so I kind of guessed you weren't from around here."

Visibly relieved, he sighed and began chuckling to himself. "No, I'm not from around this town," he said, the tone of his voice making it clear that what I had said wasn't even close to what he had meant.

He fell back into silence, and I prodded him again. "So then, where are you from? Narnia?"

He cocked his head, his hair falling in front of his eyes, and my breath caught a bit. "I do not know of this Narnia. Is it one of the nine worlds?"

"Nine?" I asked slowly. "As in the solar system?" The confused look on his face made it clear he wasn't talking celestially. "Um, it's a fantasy world, ruled by a white witch...."

His eyes lit up. "You know of Niflgard?" When I said nothing he added, "Ruled by Queen Pudani?"

I had no idea what in the world he was talking about.

"Um, no. I was talking about the book?" He looked at me blankly. "Narnia isn't a real place, it's a story," I said slowly. "There is no such thing as a white witch, right?"

He nodded quickly, his eyes growing wide with excitement. "Yes! I mean, she is not white through her magic, but it is her color in battle." He seemed to consider the words carefully. "You know of Niflgard?" he asked, and then said more to himself, "Then it's possible there *has* been communication between the realms."

I knew from watching TV that if you ran into a crazy person the worst thing you could do was try to disagree with their crazy. I knew I should just nod and walk away slowly. But again, I felt the desire to stay. I trusted him. That was the crux of it, I trusted him with no reason whatsoever. It was jarring, as it was unusual for me, yet there it was, absolute trust in him.

"You do know Narnia isn't real, right?" I began carefully. He glanced back up at me, and I felt that stare hit me again. "It's a book."

He didn't seem to get it. "A story, like a fairytale."

We stared at each other for a few seconds, each one looking as if we were waiting for the other one to say, "Just kidding!"

Neither of us said, "Just kidding."

"It's a tale about my home?" he asked when he saw I wasn't joking. "But I already said I wasn't from the ice lands."

He had that look again, as if he didn't quite understand English.

"I said fairytale," I repeated slowly.

He nodded. "Are you speaking of my home or yours, then?"

Now I looked like I didn't know English. "What?"

"You are saying it is a home tale. Are you speaking of my home or of your own?" he asked, speaking as slowly and clearly as I had.

I shook my head. "Fairytale. I'm talking about a fairytale, not a home tale."

"You said home tale twice."

I put my head down. "'Who's on First' wasn't this confusing," I mumbled to myself. I took a deep breath. "Fairy," I said, prompting him to respond.

"Home," he answered promptly.

Fairy, home. Gay, happy. What was going on here?

"What is the name of your home?" I asked.

"Faerth," he said, the word sounding so foreign rolling off his tongue.

"Okay," I said, starting over. "Repeat after me." He nodded.

"I."

"I."

"Am."

"Am."

"From."

"From."

"Fairy."

"Home."

A ha!

"You heard me saying 'home'?" I confirmed, realizing the problem.

"You didn't say that?" His voice sounded surprised and more than a little worried.

I looked at his ear and at the earring again. It didn't make any sense, but I knew somehow that earring was the cause of this confusion. I reached up toward it, but he quickly grabbed my wrist, stopping me. He wasn't rough, but it was obvious he was way stronger than I had thought.

"Trust me," I said softly.

"Why?"

His question was simple, but there was obviously a multitude of feeling behind it. It was the same question I had been asking myself. Why should I trust him? He wasn't asking about my hand or the earring or any of that. He was like a prisoner of war and was asking me why he should trust me since I was the enemy. I had no idea where that thought came from, but it seemed to fit the circumstances. At first, I didn't know how to answer him, on the surface, he had no reason to trust me. We didn't know each other, he tried to stab me, and I had no idea what I was doing here. Yet there was that bond, that feeling I was almost certain was going both ways.

My answer came to me as if I had already heard it in a dream. "Because I will never hurt you."

The grip on my wrist loosened, and I unfastened the earring from his ear. It looked like an oversized emerald that had been carved down to resemble a cat's eye. There was a glimmer, I don't know if it was from the stage lights or what, but it looked as if it had a light inside of it. The setting looked like silver with a sharp needle and fastener that screwed on the back. I felt a tingle when I put it up to my ear and slipped it in. In a fit of teenage angst, Jewel and I had had our ears pierced last summer. I had let mine close up when school started again, but the hole was still there. I felt the sharp sting of pain and then connected the back.

"So talk," I said, making sure it was in.

"I am Hawk'keen Maragold Tertania, prince and heir to the Arcadian throne." His voice was now clear and rich without a hint of accent in it.

And I knew everything he had just said was the absolute truth.

"Wait, what?" I asked in confusion.

Which was when they attacked.

CHAPTER
FIVE

HAWK had to admit he was a little smitten with the boy.

There was a poise about him that his mother would have respected even if she would also have had him killed for touching his person.

Hawk hadn't been sure what was wrong with the enchantment on the bauble, but the boy had instinctively known it to be the source of their confusion. Again, he had to wonder how much Arcadian knowledge had been lost on this side following the Abandonment? There should be no academies for The Arts, so there were no Shapers or Crafters on this side, so how Kane knew about something that looked like ordinary jewelry but wasn't remained a mystery.

He had to remember that this was not his world, and Arcadia's customs and laws did not apply. Slowly, he let his hand go and allowed Kane to remove the bauble.

The boy pricked himself when he placed the bauble in his earlobe yet barely flinched from the pain. Hawk's eyes had teared up when the Crafter had thrust the device into his lobe. His ear still felt sore almost a month later, so Kane's silent endurance seemed an impressive feat. Even more surprising was Kane's apparently calm pause for the enchantment to take hold. A slight shiver across his shoulders was the only indication that he'd felt anything at all. "So talk."

This was it.

Hawk remembered one time his father had taken him on a walk

through the halls of the main palace. As they had paced, examining the conditions of walls and flooring, the king had begun to explain to him the onus of leadership. His robes had trailed behind him as they walked; his voice was deep and commanding as befitted a lord. "Son, there comes a time in any endeavor where the risk and reward must be weighed against each other. Where you have to wonder whether what you have invested is going to be worth what you potentially get out of it and then decide right then or there what to do. In other words, do you want to fish or cut boat?"

When it was clear the older man wasn't going to elaborate on it unless questioned, Hawk had asked what the saying meant. His father explained that it meant that a leader must sometimes make the hard decisions: was it wiser to keep employing the crew of an unprofitable fishing boat in hopes that they might eventually turn a profit, or to cut the boat in half, sinking it and beginning again.

He had asked, "With the crew on it?"

"Of course," his father had replied, looking out over the vast ocean that connected to the cliffs behind the palace. "They failed in their tasks. There is no reward for failure."

It had been an eye-opening talk.

"I'm fishing," he told himself as he took a deep breath.

"I am Hawk'keen Maragold Tertania, prince and heir to the Arcadia throne." He knew the enchantment would not just translate his words into English but would convey the veracity of the statement as well. Since a literal translation would be useless in cases like this, the Crafters made sure the enchantment also carried the intent and tone of the speaker, making it an excellent tool for separating truth from fiction.

The boy was about to respond when Hawk heard them from behind.

He cursed himself as he dove for his discarded satchel. He had been so wrapped up in his and Kane's conversation he had let his guard slip. The bag lay on the ground, the top unfastened, and a trail of pens and a book on the stage. Concentrating on his blade, he called,

"Truheart" under his breath and felt the hilt of the weapon solidify in his hand. The Magics of the bag prevented anyone from finding anything that had been concealed within it unless they knew and could imagine precisely what they were reaching for. As he pulled Truheart free from its scabbard, Hawk could feel the power pulse through it, the blue glow on the blade already bright.

That meant magic.

"Behind me!" he called out to the boy, making it an order rather than a suggestion.

He was pleased to see Kane move rapidly away from the forms moving out of the shadows at them. For a second, he wondered what abominations the Dark had sent after him and then banished the thought for another time. Battle is time for action, not idle thought. He saw three uniforms move into the light and paused in surprise.

They were empty uniforms. Empty pant legs fluttering in the wind they created as they crossed the stage.

Hawk wasn't certain if the owners of the uniforms were invisible and present or being manipulated from afar, but the shirts and pants floated toward them, a sword hovering where a hand would normally clutch it tight. He didn't recognize the army battle color or regiment decorations, since none was dressed like another, but frankly, he didn't care. The Dark were sadly mistaken if they meant to impress him with that trick, and he shouted out, "For Arcadia!" and charged the first with all his strength.

Truheart flared as it sliced through the jacket, encountering no resistance. Carried by his momentum, Hawk stumbled and smacked face first to the stage floor. The coat was torn from where the heart would be all the way down to the tails, but encountering Truheart hadn't slowed the manifestation in the least. "What is this?" he exclaimed, getting to his feet.

"Hawk!" Kane called in warning as another of the floating uniforms slashed down swiftly behind him. He brought the sword up instinctively, barely parrying the blow, as he rolled away from it. The first uniform renewed its assault, focusing on the human while the second and third pressed their attack on Hawk. "Run!" he cried out as the two weapons continued to attack. It challenged every particle of training he had, but he fell back to a defensive stance. Better to maneuver the attackers so that they would stumble into and over each other, giving him an edge. And he wanted to do that. But he couldn't. Even more deeply ingrained was his duty to the innocent, and danger threatened. Blazing mad, but kept from stupidity by training, Hawk placed himself between the boy and the two bodiless uniforms that beset him.

Every swipe he made at the uniforms did nothing save tear the fabric. The weapons they wielded, on the other hand, were very real and very unstoppable.

He rolled away from them and back to his feet, blocking as well as he could, but was quickly running out of stage.

"Um." Kane's voice came from the other side of the stage. "Some help?" Hawk snapped his head around and caught a glimpse of Kane valiantly using some scraps of wood, painted brown and green, as a shield, avoiding the single enemy bent on his destruction. Hawk followed the line of Kane's stare. "By the gods!" he snapped to himself.

Another trio of uniforms had floated through the air from the other wall of the stage. The colors and medals meant nothing to him. What did mean something was the fact that he and Kane were being herded in different directions off the stage. And that was not going to happen. Abruptly, Hawk made his move.

Diving between the gap separating the coat and pants, he rolled up between Kane and the first uniform, keeping the boy behind him.

"Why are the costumes attacking us?" Kane panted, audible fear in his voice.

Hawk paused and examined them in earnest. "Costumes?" he asked over his shoulder.

"Those are for the fall play," Kane said, pointing at the first three. "And those are from *A Few Good Men*," he said, pointing at the latter trio.

Hawk had no idea what the names meant, but Kane's familiarity with them proved they were of corporeal construction, not spectral agents sent by the Dark. They were just enchantments. Hawk's battle readiness turned to rage as he realized someone was having fun at his expense.

"*Spike!*" he called out, his voice echoing across the theater.

The cat's head poked around the satchel, its eyes blinking slowly as if it was waking up.

"*Kill!*" he commanded at the same time that the creature realized they were under attack.

The Guardian reacted instantly, running at the first set of clothes as fast as he could. With each step, it grew larger, from a house cat to a panther in seconds. Its massive paws clawed through the first set effortlessly, leaving a floating set of rags instead. Undaunted, the floating weapon turned and swung at Spike.

"The weapons are enchanted! Spike, destroy them!" Hawk shouted, one hand pushing Kane back toward the wings, the other slipping his blade into his belt.

The cat's head nodded as he began to change again.

The fur melted into metallic scales; the tail fleshed out, becoming serpentine and spiked. Hawk felt Kane stop in midstep, shocked as Spike turned into a medium-sized dragonkin.

"What is…," he began to protest.

Hawk spun around and used both hands to push Kane off the stage toward the side door. "Ask later, run now!"

The uniforms had focused their attention on Spike and had formed a circle, tightening the ring around the Changeling, weapons at the ready.

Spike took half a breath as he watched his master push the boy out of the theater. Before inhaling fully he turned a quiet, dark gaze back at the uniforms.

From inside the theater came a loud roar and an odd rushing sound, followed by a clap of sound that made the doors shake. Hawk had thrown his weight against the doors, holding them shut. Seconds later, alarms began crying out all over school, and water began to spray from the ceiling's sprinklers.

"What just happened?" Kane shouted, scrambling to his feet right behind Hawk and grabbing the front of Hawk's shirt.

Kane looked as if he was ready to hit him. As much of a relief as that might have been, however, he tossed the idea away when he heard the sound of running footsteps and startled voices. People began to converge on their location.

"Excrement." Which puzzled Hawk before he realized the boy still wore the bauble.

"Shit," Hawk said, smiling proudly at him.

Kane gave him a disbelieving look and rolled his eyes. "Come on!"

He allowed himself to be pulled away as people opened the auditorium doors to find the entire stage on fire. There were cries from the adults as the other children began to shuffle out of their classrooms and out of the building.

"Where are we going?" Hawk asked, allowing Kane to lead the way.

"Outside!" he answered angrily.

"You're upset," he stated, fairly happy that he'd been able to identify the human's emotion after only a word.

Kane spun around and faced him. "Your cat-lizard thing just burned down the theater. Why would that upset me?"

Hawk considered the question quickly before carefully hazarding, "Because you wanted to destroy the enchanted garments yourself?" Kane said nothing as he turned around and exited the building.

No one noticed the small bird shoot down into the hallway, following behind them.

Half of the school wandered around outside trying to dry themselves off as smoke billowed out of the theater doors. The other half divided its time either staring and talking or staring and not talking and watching the building burn. Kane dragged Hawk away from the crowd to a spot near a small grove of trees. After making sure they were alone he asked, "Why did you burn down the theater?" His tone wasn't as angry, but it was obvious he was upset.

If Hawk had any illusions that the boy might know something of The Arts, his question dispelled them. Hawk paused as he mulled the question. "Because the uniforms would have come at us endlessly as long as their weapons remained intact. Magical fire is the quickest way to destroy weapons of that nature."

"You burned the theater down!"

Hawk narrowed his eyes. "You said that already." He reached for the bauble. "Is it broken?"

Kane slapped his hand as he exclaimed, "You can't just go burning places to the ground!"

Hawk rubbed his hand. "Don't exaggerate, the structure is still standing!" As he finished, part of the roof crashed in; the crowd screamed in surprise. "Well, it is for now."

Kane rolled his eyes and looked away from him for a moment.

"It wasn't a particularly good theater, you know," he offered, trying to soften the pain.

"*Yes, it was!*" Kane exploded, turning back to him. "It was a perfectly serviceable theater, and it was ours!" And then in a whispered hiss, "And you burned it down!"

Hawk paused and then corrected him. "Actually, I ordered it to be burnt down. I didn't actually take flame to it." When he saw the anger in Kane's face he added, "Well, there is a difference."

"So you had your… thing burn it down! It's still a pile of ashes!"

"Guardian," Hawk amended.

Kane paused before asking, "That cat thing is your Guardian?"

"I'm a Changeling," a voice called from above them. "Not a cat thing." Kane peered up and spotted the black cat sitting on a low branch, the satchel in its claws. It dropped the bag down to Hawk and told him, "They're gone."

Hawk nodded, pulled Truheart off his belt, and put it back inside. "Excellent."

"The cat talks?" Kane asked, obviously at the edge of his tolerance.

"I speak Faerth," the cat answered and then looked at Hawk. "How can he understand me?"

Hawk held the bag open and motioned for the Changeling to jump into it.

Spike sighed and answered his own question as he readied himself for the drop. "Because he's wearing the bauble. Of course he is because, when we were told to stay as invisible as possible, that meant unless you fancy a boy. In that case, do whatever you damn well please."

With perfect form it jumped off the branch and toward the bag.

Hawk moved the bag to the left. The cat hit the ground with a humiliating thud. Spike looked at him, slightly dazed as Hawk said, "I'm sorry. All that sarcasm affected my aim. Care to try again?"

This time Spike stayed silent as he leapt into the bag.

Hawk closed and fastened it shut and looked up to find Kane just staring at him in what could only be befuddlement. "Who are you?" the human finally asked.

"I answered that already," he said, reaching up and snatching back the bauble from Kane's ear and catching the jewel with his other hand. "There is a girl approaching us," Hawk said, slipping the bauble into his earlobe.

"What?" Kane asked, not understanding anything that was happening around him.

"Girl," Hawk whispered as he spun Kane around to face her.

Jewel looked at him, her concern was thinly veiled by annoyance. "Are you okay?"

Kane nodded, still slightly in shock. "Yeah, we're fine," he answered.

"We?" she asked. Whatever anger she still felt about Kane pushing her dispelled itself under a wave of concern.

Kane nodded and looked behind him. "Yeah, me and—of course you're gone." The last part said to himself.

"You're acting weird," she said as Kane scanned as far as he could see, trying to spot Hawk.

But he had vanished. Again.

CHAPTER
SIX

IF HE had been there, I would have blown up at him.

I could totally tell that Jewel had still been mad at me when she walked up, but that didn't last since I sounded like a complete crazy person talking about someone who wasn't there. Jewel knew the proper protocol when dealing with crazy people, of course. When I told her that the guy she was sure didn't exist had just been here next to me and was now gone, she nodded and, very calmly, asked me if I wanted to sit down.

I hated Hawk even more.

In silence we all watched as the theater burned down. Ms. Brody cried on the lawn like her firstborn had been trapped inside the auditorium. I pinched the bridge of my nose and managed not to say anything. Since we were a bunch of freaks, a few kids cried also. Some joined hands and sang the spirit of the theater to the hereafter.

Hand to God? I felt like puking. Bad enough they were going to get weepy over a building, but to chant its soul to theater heaven was too much.

"I'm leaving," I announced, getting to my feet. I had always disliked Athens, but this, this was going too far into the weeds of weird. This had been a fire, a *real* fire, where someone could have been hurt, and we were chanting?

"You can't," Jewel said, rising with me. "We're supposed to stay here."

I went to grab my backpack and realized it wasn't with me. I slapped my forehead and groaned. "Oh dammit; it was in there."

Jewel did a double take as she realized what I had just said. "You were in the theater?"

I froze, stuck between the instant impulse to just lie to her and the stronger impulse to tell her everything because, God knew, I needed someone to talk to.

"Kane," Jewel whispered to me. "Did you burn the theater down?"

The question sounded a lot to me like an accusation, and I yanked away from her. "Yes, Jewel. I was pretty sure if someone dropped pig's blood on me nothing would happen, so I was in there practicing how to light things on fire like every good Stephen King character should."

I could see my words had cut her as deeply as hers had cut me when she glared back at me. This was the first actual fight we'd ever had, and neither one of us knew how to deal with it. She knew something was up, and I wasn't talking. I always talked, talking made our friendship work. I had lashed out at her with the cynical words I normally reserved for others, and she grew cold in reaction. "Well, for all I know, your imaginary boyfriend lit it on fire."

"No, it was his magic cat thing," I blurted out and rushed past her.

What was left of the rational part of my brain knew that I wasn't really mad at Jewel. I was mad that, twenty-four hours earlier, my life made sense. True, completely shitty sense, but sense nonetheless. And then I'd seen *him*. Ever since he'd passed me in the hall, my life had taken a left turn into the woods. I wasn't sure I was ever going to find my way out again, and that pissed me off even more.

Strange hot guys, baubles that were lie detectors on the side, magic uniforms, and a talking cat-dragon thing that could burn down a building; I'd reached the limit of things I couldn't understand but was forced to accept for one day, so I just left. Jewel didn't say anything as I marched off the lawn.

The school was in such a panic it was just a matter of walking off campus as more firemen rushed toward the blaze. The winds were kicking up, and what had started as small fire was threatening to take down more than just the auditorium. I didn't know if Hawk or Jewel was following me, and I didn't care. Elvis has left the building, and I didn't know if he was coming back or not.

Every person in town walked or biked or drove past me, heading toward the school; the black smoke rising into the air was visible for miles. And it was probably the most exciting thing that had happened in Athens, Iowa, for years.

The farther I retreated from school, the quieter the world became. The sidewalk was covered with leaves as the winds tore down my street from behind. I hurried up to my house to escape the chill as fast as I could.

I wasn't too surprised to see my front door open before I could pull out my keys to unlock it. "Your window lock is sorely deficient."

I stalked past Hawk, who held the door open, and saw what I assumed was his cat thing sitting on my couch. At least I hoped what I saw was his cat thing since there was a black furry monkey calmly holding our TV remote sitting there.

"My window is two stories up with no way to get close to it, so we weren't really expecting anyone to jimmy the lock." I grabbed the remote out of the creature's hand and turned the TV off. It looked up and hissed at me in anger and, in a fit of mental exhaustion, I hissed back at it.

I could swear the thing looked like it was going to rip out my throat, then I heard Hawk behind me telling the creature, "Spike, go away."

Spike said something back, making the same sound I'd assume a dog would make if it tried to speak French. Whatever it said, it wasn't good, because Hawk's face grew stern as he barked, "Spike. Out. *Now!*"

The monkey thing slinked off the couch, morphing back to the cat as it bounded up the stairs. "That thing doesn't like me," I said, when I was pretty sure it was out of earshot.

"No, he doesn't," Hawk said, sitting in my father's chair with an exhausted sigh.

That took me aback for a moment. "Wait, why doesn't he like me? What did I do?"

He smiled up at me. "You didn't do anything, it is most likely because of me."

I brushed off the couch, making sure I didn't sit in any monkey-cat poo. "I'm confused."

Hawk nodded as I waited for him to add something. After a few seconds I kicked the chair. "So explain!"

He sighed as he moved his legs out of the way in case the next time I kicked it was at him instead of the chair. "That would take some time."

"I have time," I said, not breaking eye contact.

"Do you have sustenance?" he asked, apparently completely un-phased by my anger.

"Do I have… you mean food?"

"And drink," he added. "Combat magic leaves me drained."

Magic? I'd love to call him crazy, but his talking cat-lizard-monkey thing didn't like me and it was most likely up in my room pissing on my stuff.

"Do you eat meat?" I asked, getting up and crossing to the kitchen.

"Of course, why wouldn't I?" he asked, turning around in the chair.

"It's a weird town, not everyone eats the same thing," I said, opening the fridge and grabbing the leftovers from Dad's and my supper.

I saw him pulling off his boots and tried not to stare because I suddenly wanted to see his bare feet. What the hell was wrong with me? "They eat food, correct?" he called to me.

I tossed a little bit of everything on a plate and began to nuke it. "Well, vegetarians don't eat red meat. Vegans eat less than that. There are a couple of people that only eat natural things, meaning no processed sugar or preservatives or...." I looked over, and he was standing next to me. His physical presence was intimidating but not threatening. The light from the living room gleamed off his hair in a way that made it almost glow for a moment. He was so damn pretty it hurt.

"You know I understand maybe every third word, correct?" he asked with that damn infuriating grin.

I felt myself literally swoon, I was standing so near him. I mean, an actual swoon where I put a hand on one of the kitchen chairs so I didn't topple forward into him. He opened his mouth to say something, no doubt to tease me about my reaction, when something popped in the microwave.

Fascinated, he knelt down and peered in the window.

"It is a type of oven?" he asked as he tapped the glass with his finger. I winced at how close he was to it and pulled him back. "Yeah, microwaves. Good for cooking, bad for staring at."

He allowed me to move him, but it was obvious from the set of his shoulders that if he didn't want to budge, I'd need a bulldozer to get him in motion. "It's dangerous?"

"Kinda," I said, reluctantly letting go of him.

"Kinda?" he asked, the word sounding like an entirely different language coming from his mouth.

I sighed and held my hand out. He laughed as he unfastened the earring and placed it on my palm. I slipped it in and looked at him. "Kinda."

His smile got wider as he exclaimed, "Of sorts!" And then tried again. "Kinda." He looked at me. "Kinda?"

I nodded. "You're saying it right."

His head cocked slightly. "I can't tell if you're telling the truth anymore. That sounded like a convenient lie."

I touched the earring as I asked, "It's a lie detector?"

He nodded. "Part of the spell."

"Spell?" I asked. "As in magic?"

"So you do know of it." He sat down, somehow making our old kitchen table look five times more valuable by just leaning on it. "Is it still taught somewhere?"

"Magic?" I asked, trying to rein in my disbelief. He nodded. "Magic doesn't exist," I spluttered.

He stared at me for almost five seconds before bursting out laughing. Make that guffawing. He pounded the table as his bare feet slapped against the floor. I didn't see what was so funny, which made him laugh harder. What had been *kinda* amusing at first, faded, and I began to suspect Hawk had found an excuse to laugh at me. Grim faced, I asked over his braying, "What's so funny?"

Face red with mirth, eyes glistening with tears he'd been laughing so hard, he tried to say something. "You... you're...." He gasped between erupting chuckles. "You're wearing a magic bauble, and you claim that magic doesn't exist." Which sent him off into another fit of laughter. "I knew humans lived in denial, but I never dreamed—"

The bell went off on the microwave and that brought his attention back quickly. He stared suspiciously at the machine after he dried his eyes on his sleeve. The speed with which he went from utterly silly to dangerously focused startled me. "The oven chirped," he said, attempting to sober himself up. Little hiccups of laughter escaped every few seconds despite his best efforts at keeping his lips tightly pressed together.

"Food's done," I said, popping the microwave door open and pulling out the hot plate. I set it down in front of him, and he marveled at the steam coming off of it.

"It's burning up," he remarked, examining the plate from all sides and then, after tapping the rim to check for heat, lifting it up and peering underneath. "The plate is not enchanted?"

"The oven heats things up," I explained, grabbing a couple of forks from the silverware drawer. "The food, the plate, everything. Here." I handed him a fork, watched him tap the food with the tines.

"What is this?" he asked, picking at the food.

"All I have to eat," I said, digging in. He watched me swallow and then took a bite himself. At first he nibbled hesitantly and then he began chewing in earnest. His eyes widened, and he nodded as he took another bite enthusiastically. "This is good!" he said, talking through a mouthful. His exuberance was infectious, and I found myself laughing with him.

"I've never seen anyone so pleased with leftovers," I said.

He stopped in midbite. "Scraps?"

I wasn't sure what he was talking about until I remembered I still had the earring on. Leftovers translated as scraps in a weird sideways logic, so I nodded. "Close enough. This is what my father and I didn't finish last night."

He spat the food in his mouth across the room as he shoved his chair away from the table so he could stand.

Surprised, and not sure what had happened, I dropped my fork and pushed away from the table also. The table jerked, and the plate fell to the ground, shattering. "What?"

"You dared to feed me table scraps?" he raged. Even furious he was handsome, the way his features became sharper, and his eyes narrowed in anger. Where I should be concerned, I was just turned on. It was cosmically unfair.

"*Dare?*" I screamed back. "It's food, you jackass! You were liking it just fine before you spit it up like a freaking child!"

His eyes widened in fury. "I am the heir of the nine worlds, prince of Arcadia and holder of the right of ascens—"

"*Hawk!*" Spike bellowed from the kitchen entrance. I spun, startled at the sound. The creature was standing at the doorway to the kitchen, his face grim, reminding me of a teacher who had caught a student goofing off.

I glanced back and saw the absolute chagrin in Hawk's expression as he slowly closed his mouth. A silent conversation passed between the creature and Hawk, and it was obvious Hawk was getting his ass kicked. He looked down at the spilt food and looked, for a moment, mortified. "I am…," he said in an absent tone, like he was talking to himself. Then he looked up at me. "I apologize," he said, putting a hand over his heart, almost as if he was saluting me. "I was your guest, and I behaved abhorrently."

His words were so formal now they were painful.

"I shall leave," he said, edging around the table and into the living room. He jerked his boots on, and Spike stepped around toward him, his feline paws morphing into hands to assist Hawk. "I have this," I heard him say. "Find him compensation for my breach of etiquette."

I could see the very human intelligence in those cat eyes as Spike shot a glare over at me before slinking off to the knapsack. He dug around inside it while Hawk tightened the straps on his boots, every motion chopped and echoing his anger. After a few seconds, I saw the thing pass his master something before it bundled the sack back up.

Hawk turned toward me, his face as expressionless as a statue. There was no warmth in his eyes as he looked at me and made a half bow. "I humbly apologize for my behavior. Please accept this as payment for your kindness and patience." He handed me a ruby the size of a baseball, cut into what looked like a tiny Death Star. The living room light caught it and I saw what I suspected were words engraved inside the rock's core. As I watched, they floated across one of the broad facets of the ruby as the light shifted.

Hawk glanced up, still bent in that bow, the ruby in his hand extended toward me. He realized I'd made no move to take the enormous rock. "Is this not satisfactory?" He stood quickly and snapped his fingers. Spike started toward him with the bag in hand.

"No!" I cried out, stopping both of them. "I mean yes, it's great, but I don't want it. It's too much."

He seemed puzzled, looking back toward the jewel that had to be bigger than the Hope Diamond and then to me. "Then take it for payment."

"For what?" I asked, still not daring to get near the thing.

"For the meal and the servants that will have to clean it up," he explained.

"*I* have to clean it up," I said frankly.

"Oh." He seemed embarrassed for me. "Well, then take it for... um... your work then." When I refused to touch the gem, he set it down on the coffee table. "My apologies again," he said, moving toward the door.

I tried to intercept him. "Hawk! Why are you leaving?"

He looked back at me and held my gaze for a long, hard, few seconds. "Because I don't belong here."

"You don't have to go," I pleaded. "I can order new food!" I hated that I sounded so needy.

"It isn't the food," he replied back, facing me. His voice sounded almost wistful as he said, "Good-bye, Kane." There was no emotion on his face, but I knew it wasn't to be trusted. I just knew that if he was a prince he'd been schooled on how to keep his emotions unreadable.

He opened the door and pulled his jacket free of my grasp. Then, never once looking back, he strode down our walkway. Spike followed him a few feet and then turned back and looked at me. It's hard to tell with a cat, but I could swear he was silently laughing at me.

As Hawk reached the sidewalk I saw Jewel hurrying toward my house from the other direction. When she saw him, she paused, her expression of shock visible from where I stood at the door of my house. Hawk nodded at her as he walked by; I noticed Spike was nowhere to be seen. After Hawk passed her, she looked at me, pointed at him as she mouthed, "Is that him?" I suddenly felt cold, as if part of me were leaving with him.

She scurried up the walk, glancing a few times over her shoulder at him. "Oh, crap, he *is* hot! And real!" I raised an eyebrow at her and she shot me a glance. "Oh, please, I had money he was either a huge rabbit only you could see or a leprechaun that was going to tell you to burn stuff."

I didn't laugh as he turned the corner and disappeared.

"So what was he doing here?" she asked.

I had to admit to myself, I still had no idea.

CHAPTER SEVEN

"OH MY God! He's real?" Jewel exclaimed instead of asking as she rushed into the house.

I nodded and sat down in my dad's chair. It was still vaguely warm from where Hawk had sat.

"And he is *hot!*" she said again for emphasis, pacing the living room in nervous excitement. "And he goes to our school?" I nodded again. "Really? Does he have a cloak of invisibility or something?"

I laughed to myself as I said, "You have no idea."

She heard the tone of my voice and paused. "What's wrong? You had the hottest guy in the... well, *ever* in your house, and you're bummed?" She didn't even give me time to form a response much less answer as she went on, "Oh, is he homophobic? Did he get mad when you hit on him?" Another non-pause. "Did you hit on him? Oh my God! Did you kiss him?" She clapped her hands in glee. "Is he a good kisser?"

She looked at me, clearly wanting an answer, so I just waited for her to take a breath.

"Done?" I asked, raising one eyebrow at her. She nodded. "He isn't a homophobe, I wasn't flirting with him, and we didn't kiss."

She waited for me to go on, but I just sat there, hoping there was a point to what she was saying.

"Why not?" she called out as she walked toward me to slap the top of my head. She went to swing at me and I winced away from the impending blow. Jewel might be a girl, but she packed one hell of a wallop when she wanted to.

I heard a voice say, "Protect" from behind her at the same instant I saw the jewel on the table flash brightly. She went flying back onto the carpet. I opened my other eye, and we both looked at each other in shock. Then she began to laugh. "Did I just trip on nothing?"

I glanced over at the gem. It had returned to normal ruby coloring. On any other day, I would have wondered if I had imagined Jewel taking a flying leap, but after the talking cat thing, being stabbed with a knife that didn't leave a wound, and wearing an earring that let you understand languages, a glowing ruby that takes offense to slaps was just not weird enough for me.

I laughed the best I could and got up to help her to her feet. As I passed the table, I kneed the edge, knocking the ruby off toward the couch. It made an audible thud as it hit the floor.

"What was that?" she asked as I pulled her up.

"Old house," I replied quickly. "Makes a lot of weird noises."

She looked confused. "I never heard that before."

"My dad's gone. Lack of white noise makes everything louder," I added, sitting down on the couch, covering the gem with my feet.

"Right," she said, suddenly remembering. "My mom wanted you to come over for dinner tonight since you're pulling a Macaulay Culkin for the week."

I rolled my eyes. "Why does everyone think I'm *Home Alone* all of a sudden?"

That same voice came from between my feet saying, "The comparison of a young boy left alone during the holidays being juxtaposed against you being left alone for the first time in your life is a viable popular cultural reference." I kicked the gem under the couch as I waited for Jewel to comment on my new talking rock.

Instead, she shrugged as if she heard nothing and said, "I dunno, but it has to beat take-out," she said glancing over at the kitchen table, seeing the broken plate on the ground. "Kane, what happened?"

Her question didn't even register with me; I was too engrossed in wondering how she could not have heard those words. She snapped her fingers at me. "Kane! What happened in the kitchen?"

"Nothing," I said, getting up, moving to enter the kitchen before she could. I grabbed a broom and dustpan from the cellar stairway as Jewel kept talking.

"Did he do this?" Her voice was angry, and I could tell she'd begun to craft another little soap opera in her head. "Did he throw it at you? Is he Greek? Greek guys are hot but they can be dicks. Kane, you have to be careful with him because Greek guys have tempers."

As I swept up the mess I said, "He's not Greek." But I knew it was a waste of time.

"I think they are like the guys on *Jersey Shore*." She was now just talking to herself. "No wait, those are Italians." She looked back at me. "Is he Italian? With that dark hair and those dreamy blue eyes, he could be. Have you seen him with his shirt off? Is he hairy? Because if he's hairy he's Italian." She paused. "Or Greek, I think they are hairy too. Is he hairy?"

I lost it.

On any other day, I could take this kind of banter. Normally, I'd be the same kind of brainless chatterbox. After all, all we used to do was talk about nothing and dream about what life was like outside of Athens in conversations that sounded like Jewel's current babble. But today, today was different. I felt like I was forty years old and working on my last nerve as I snapped, "Don't you ever shut up?"

She froze, the same look on her face as when I pushed her in the hallway.

"He isn't homophobic. We didn't kiss. I didn't see him with his shirt off, and he isn't Greek, Italian, or any other nationality you'd know. Can we please talk about something else?"

Her shock faded and scorn replaced the startled expression on her face. "Well excuse me, Mr. Pyromaniac. I guess I'm not good enough to hear about your new boyfriend."

"He's not my—" I tried to interject but she just rolled on.

"I came here to tell you about dinner. I'll just tell my mom you're too good to eat with us." She spun on her heels and marched out the door. Part of me wanted to call out to her and apologize, but I honestly did not have the energy. Instead, I threw the broken plate in the trash and let the broom drop to the kitchen floor.

I collapsed into my dad's chair, wishing he was home. Then I was glad he wasn't here because he'd just be another person I couldn't talk to about the insanity that was Hawk. "Why does this have to be so hard?" I asked out loud.

"Because without adversity there is no natural selection possible, inviting an inferior creation." The voice came from underneath the couch.

I knelt down and felt for the voice's owner with one hand. I pulled it out along with a dust bunny the size of my head and vowed that we needed to clean better. Holding it up to my face, I studied it close up. There was some kind of inner light inside, like a candle was somehow contained in it, so I wasn't losing my mind. What was amazing, though, were the letters that swirled around the circumference of the core, seemingly carved into the gem itself. They floated by, and I thought I was just able to make out what they were spelling, but the more I tried to concentrate on them, the harder it became. My head began to ache like I had eaten ice cream too quickly as I squinted, really looking inside. "Why can't I read them?" I exclaimed.

"Because the enchantment on the bauble does not allow for the deciphering of arcane symbols. It serves only to facilitate normal communication." The voice was pleasant and sounded vaguely British.

"My enchantment?" I echoed, as the last shred of common sense I possessed checked out for the night. Literally nothing was going to surprise me anymore. Ever.

"More specifically, the enchantment placed on the earring you wear."

I almost asked what he was talking about when I remembered I still had Hawk's earring. I felt its warm surface between my fingers and realized Hawk had taken off without remembering I had it.

"He can't understand English without this," I exclaimed, suddenly worried.

"No, he cannot," the gem agreed.

I looked back at it suspiciously. "Why are you answering everything I ask?"

I could swear the gem's voice became boastful as it said, "I am the Raatnaraj Ruber Scientia, first consular to the Stone Throne and was a personal gift to the royal family of Arcadia by the Djupur himself."

"Ruber?" Not wanting to ask the stone what any of that meant because the gem seemed so proud of it that it might be taken as an insult.

"You may refer to me as that, yes."

"Okay, Ruber, why are you talking?" I settled back, the sense that Ruber's response might be longer than ten words.

The ruby made a slight noise that sounded a lot like a hummmpph before answering. "To answer it in a way that you would understand, I am a life form that instead of flesh and blood is composed of minerals. I am a gem elemental, if you will."

"Living ruby, got it." I nodded.

I saw the letters pause for a moment and had the feeling I was on the receiving end of a withering stare from the talking rock. "I was in direct line of succession for the throne, I'll have you know. I am not just a 'living ruby'," it answered.

"Gems have thrones?"

"Well, not thrones as you know them, but we do have a hierarchy, yes," it explained.

"Wait, so there are living gemstones where Hawk comes from, and you were a royal one?" I summarized.

"Not from Hawk's world per se, but one connected to his, yes.

Hence my title." Its voice was almost literally dripping with condescension.

"Okay, so you're saying that rubies are in charge? What about diamonds?"

I swore the temperature in the room dropped forty degrees. "Diamonds are excessively pampered, ignorant inbreds that rule only because of tradition. I assure you, anything a diamond can do a ruby can do better, and with color I might add."

That was it. I just insulted a talking rock.

"I'm sorry," I said, feeling foolish. "Diamonds suck, you're right. You're a prince or something?"

"That word would work, yes," Ruber said.

"So then how does a prince get traded to someone else and then end up in Hawk's backpack?"

Another pause, and I felt if the stone had a face and could have moved, it would have turned away from me as it answered, "That is a long and sordid tale."

"Is it a long and sordid tale you need to tell right now?" I asked, stifling a yawn.

"Of course not," the gem said, obviously insulted.

"This has just been a day," I replied, amid another yawn. "And I need some sleep before I pass out."

"Of course," Ruber said, floating up from the table.

"Oh wow. You can fly," I said, amazed.

"I am capable of many tasks," the ruby answered smugly.

"Bully for you," I said, walking up the stairs to my room. "Hey, can you find out where he is staying so I can give this back?" My room was lit with a magical red glow as Ruber floated in.

"I am aware of that location, yes," he said, settling down on my dresser.

I pulled my shirt off and fell onto my bed. "Awesome. We can do that tomorrow," I mumbled into my pillow as I fell asleep.

HAWK threw the pack across the room as he walked into the house.

"Dammit!" Hawk exclaimed as he fumed, pacing the room.

"Master?" Spike mewed, the combination of normal cat sounds and the cadence of his other-world-self combining well enough.

"That boy is…," he growled, kicking the floor in anger. "I had every right to refuse scraps!" he bellowed.

"Of course you did, master," Spike agreed, following behind him. "The human has no knowledge of the way things are." After a beat. "We should kill him now."

"*Enough with the killing!*" Hawk roared, spinning on the Changeling. "We are not killing anyone without cause, and that boy has not given any cause. Are we clear?"

"But he has…," Spike began to argue.

"*Are we clear?*" Hawk boomed the question again.

"Yessir," Spike said in a tiny voice.

"Dammit!" he said again, sitting down on the bedroll he used to sleep on. "Why did I react like that?" he asked himself aloud. "And why do I care about it?"

WHEN I got up, there was a message on the answering machine saying that school was closed for today and would most likely open again Monday. I felt guilty for loving the fact that we got a three-day weekend because Hawk burned the place down. As soon as I thought about him I felt a hole in my chest where he was supposed to be. As I stood in the shower I tried to distance myself from the feeling, knowing there was no way it could be real.

This was just emotional residue based on a lifetime of isolation. I didn't even know him, so how could I feel this much? I had heard tales of teenage puppy love and always dismissed them, mostly because I knew I was never going to find love until I left for college. I swore to myself I would never be that guy, the guy who loses his shit for the first pretty face he sees.

And yet my shit was truly lost.

I got dressed, wondering all the while if I should go and find him or not. I supposed I could ask Ruber to take him the earring, but I wanted to see him again. I grabbed a pillow off my bed and screamed into it as I fought the dueling urges in my heart. I wanted to be all Destiny's Child and be an independent woman.

But I needed to see him more.

"Come on, Ruber," I said, grabbing my satchel and slipping it over my shoulder. "Show me where Hawk is."

"Indubitably, sir," it said, floating in front of me as I walked out the door.

HAWK opened his eyes and found two iridescently gold eyes staring back at him.

"Are you awake yet?" Spike, in the form of the black cat, asked.

Hawk sighed, dislodging the "cat" as he turned over. "Go away, Spike."

Undaunted, Spike moved around to Hawk's face. "The sun is up, though, and you are normally awake by then."

"It's called morning, and you know that," Hawk said, flopping over the other way. "I hate it when you play helpless little kitten."

Spike prowled down Hawk's back and over his lower legs, finally ending up looking back into his face. "You're upset."

Hawk stared off across the floor as he mumbled expressionlessly, "I'm sad."

Spike inched forward a little more. "Because of the human." Hawk nodded. "Please don't be sad because of the boy. He's...."

Hawk's eyes locked onto Spike's, and the Changeling knew he had to choose his next words carefully. "...not worth your sorrow?" he tried.

Hawk sighed, wriggling until he ended up on his back. He propped his head up with his hands and stared at the cracks in the ceiling. "Not worth it. I don't even know what that means anymore."

Spike crept cautiously up onto his master's chest and, when Hawk made no move to brush him off, began to knead his front two paws slowly. "You are a prince, heir to the throne of Arcadia. You can have any person in existence, why care about a lowly human?"

"He's not lowly," Hawk said, his voice dropping an octave in growing anger.

"He's a commoner. He fed you scraps and was going to clean the floor himself. How is that in any way not lower than you?"

Hawk's eyes flashed in anger as he reached out and grabbed the scruff of the Changeling's neck. "He's not lowly."

Spike froze, his form shrinking to that of a kitten in response. "I'm sorry?" he offered.

Hawk tossed him aside, the kitten becoming a sparrow and landing in the long-disused fireplace. Wisely, he didn't say anything else as Hawk settled back into his funk.

They stayed that way for another half hour, Hawk mulling his thoughts as Spike kept a respectful distance.

The sound of the door opening cracked like a gunshot in the silence.

Both of them acted as one. Spike leaped off the mantel, his black feathers flattening together, becoming a pelt of black fur covering what was now a vicious dire wolf. Hawk grabbed Truheart, which had lain within hand's reach on the bed all night, rolled off his bed, and came to his feet in one movement. His teeth were set as he stared at the opening door. Startled, on one level, he realized he was in the mood for a fight.

The door stopped at about a quarter open and a head peeked around the side to check the interior. Spike leapt as Hawk screamed for him to stop.

There was a pulse of red light as Ruber faded into visibility, expanding his field to repel the wolf. Spike flew back, rolling up onto his haunches almost instantly, his claws digging into the rotted wooden floor to stop his momentum. Hawk called at him to stop again but the Changeling was obviously enraged. He charged at Kane, who stood at the doorway, a stunned look on his face. The wolf's snout grew longer as the fur shimmered into a layer of scaled skin. What started its jump as a wolf hit the middle of the leap as a large velociraptor. Kane screamed and drew back, but Ruber was not impressed by the transformation.

The gem swung in a wide circle around the lizard and collided into the side of its head, knocking him down and away from Kane. Screeching its anger, the dinosaur slid across the floor, scrambling with its claws to stop itself. The lizard shrank and twisted to feline form as he reoriented himself, focusing back at Kane. Ruber darted between Kane and the jaguar, a low hum beginning to form from inside of the ruby.

Spike let out a deafening roar and crouched for the attack again.

Which was when Hawk barged in front of him and glowered down at him. He still held his sword in one hand; his expression had gone beyond furious. "If you move one more inch toward him I will personally cut off your head," he vowed.

Spike sidled to the left, attempting to look around Hawk, but the prince would not get out of its face. "I mean it, Spike. Stand. Down. *Now!*"

The Changeling continued to growl for another few seconds as its form began to shrink. Now the black cat again, he looked up at Ruber, his eyes more predatory than ever.

"Go upstairs," Hawk ordered, his stance not relaxing a micron.

"They are intruders—" Spike began to argue.

Hawk casually swung the sword toward the cat, effortlessly stopping the motion a hairsbreadth from its neck. "I mean it. Go."

Cursing inaudibly, Spike moved around the human and ruby,

slinking its way up the stairs, casting furious glances behind him as he went.

Only when he was out of sight did Hawk relax. He let out a sigh and turned back to Kane. "You have quite an effect on him," he said with a small smile.

Kane didn't move as he looked at the stairs and then back to the large gashes carved out of the floor where the velociraptor had skidded. Words apparently didn't want to cooperate with him; he opened and closed his mouth helplessly.

"Are you okay?" Hawk asked worriedly.

"He was just attacked by a Changeling," Ruber said, closing the door behind Kane. "I am quite sure that is outside of the normal range of events in his life."

Hawk shot a dirty look at the gem as he led Kane over to a chair and sat him down. "We weren't expecting people to find us. Spike didn't mean anything by it."

Kane looked up at him. "You can't be that stupid." Hawk pulled back a bit, confused. "Let me spell it out for you. That thing wanted to kill me. He still wants to kill me!" he exclaimed loudly.

"No, he doesn't," Hawk tried to assure him.

"Yes, I do." The voice came from the second floor.

"*Shut up!*" Hawk roared at the ceiling.

Kane shook his head and held out his hand to Hawk. "Anyways, I came to give you this. You forgot it." Hawk put his hand up to his ear and realized he hadn't even noticed.

He took it slowly. "Thank you, I would have been…." His words trailed off as he put it in his ear. "Well, it would have been bad."

Kane noticed the other boy was shirtless and looked away quickly. "Um, so… this is where you live?" he asked, standing up and looking anywhere but at the half-naked boy.

"It's not—" Hawk said, looking around in embarrassment. He quickly began throwing his clothes into a corner, out of sight. "It was the only abandoned house we could find," he explained awkwardly as he pulled a shirt on. He kicked the blanket off his bed and behind the chair.

"No it's... rustic," Kane said, trying to be as nice as possible.

Hawk raised one eyebrow skeptically. "It's a hovel."

"Yeah, it's pretty bad," Kane agreed, laughing.

Hawk tried not to notice the way he reacted to the sound of Kane's laughter.

"So. You brought the bauble to me," he said self-consciously.

"Yeah," Kane agreed, looking around some more. "I guess... I should go, right?"

Hawk answered quickly, "You don't have to go." Clearing his throat he added. "I mean, if you don't want to."

Kane answered just as rapidly. "No, I'm fine."

"Because we don't have to stay here."

"If you don't want to stay here...," Kane countered.

"No, I'm fine."

"Fine."

"Fine."

Finally Ruber said, "Oh dear God, please just admit you like each other and move on to the next step."

Both boys blushed as they looked at each other and then away.

"What is there to do in your world?" Hawk said, deciding to pierce the silence.

"In general?" Kane asked, confused.

"In this town," Hawk clarified.

"Oh. Oh! Well... with no school we can go get coffee. Or see a movie."

"Movie?" Hawk asked, the word obviously having no direct translation.

"Um... moving pictures. Like...." He looked at Ruber. "Little help?"

"It's a form of entertainment," the ruby described, sounding bored. "Like a play that has been recorded and replayed."

Hawk was obviously intrigued. "A play that has been frozen and then thawed somewhere else?"

"Well... no... well, close enough," Kane decided aloud. "You want to go?"

"With you?"

"If you want to, I mean, you don't have to...," Kane began to stammer.

"Yes, together," Ruber said, cutting him off. Kane tried to shush the ruby with a look.

"I'd love to go with you," Hawk said, smiling. "To the movies. I mean," he added. "I mean, I love the movie, or I might if it...."

"Please. Stop talking," Ruber announced before Hawk could go on.

"Let me put on my boots," Hawk finished, giving the gem an angry glare.

I'M NOT sure how you can get turned on watching someone put on shoes, but I was.

He looked so embarrassed to be squatting in any house, much less a dusty one with no running anything... it just broke my heart. He seemed so lost that it took everything I had not to just rush over to him and tell him it was going to be okay. Of course, I had no idea if things were going to be okay, since I had no idea what was going on. I knew I should have been more freaked out by the whole magic ruby and the vicious Changeling thing, but they were just part of Hawk's world.

And that world was one I wanted to be a part of, I realized. I didn't even know if my being part of his life was possible. But I knew that, if being a part of his life wasn't possible in the end, I wanted to be close to him as long as I could.

"I am ready," he said from behind me.

He looked perfect.

Between the way his shirt tightened across his chest and his jeans hugged his ass, he looked like he had been pampered by a team of make-up artists instead of having just rolled out of bed.

Literally rolled out of bed.

"Is there something wrong with the way I am dressed?" he asked after seeing my Double Take and Drool session.

I shook my head and looked away again. "You're fine. I mean, they're fine. I mean… yes. You're dressed perfectly." Nice work, Kane. Stumble over that tongue much?

He shot me a smile that made me embarrassed and excited all at once.

"You look incredib—" he started to say when Spike bounded down the steps.

"Are we leaving?" he asked Hawk eagerly. Seeing a cat talk is weird. It's nothing like the Disney cartoons where the cat's entire face reflected human expressions. Spike's mouth moved like a human's, but the rest of his cat face was as inexpressive as any feline I'd ever seen.

"*We* are," Hawk said, indicating himself and me. "*You* are staying here."

"Why?" he whined.

"You shouldn't even have to ask that." His voice was full of contempt toward Spike, and I felt a little sorry for him.

That was right up until the cat turned back at me and showed me what a cat's face would look like if he hated every little thing about you and wished you were dead. Nothing Disney about that, either, by the way.

"Do not blame him!" Hawk said, causing Spike to look away quickly. "You brought this upon yourself. Stay here and clean up this mess," he ordered as he shepherded me out the door. "Do something useful."

I looked back as the door was closing, and Spike's feelings came through pretty clearly to me. That Changeling hated my guts.

I noticed that the air was colder than normal as we walked the streets of Athens. My dad's storm was on its way, and he was halfway across the country missing it. Hawk looked around at everything. Even strolling casually he had a presence that made it pretty clear he wasn't from around town. He asked questions about everything, and seemed to be the most interested in what the various stores sold and how they came to be named what they were.

"Puns?" he asked after I tried explaining.

"Wordplay. Um, jokes about...," I started to explain.

"I know what a pun is," he interrupted me with a grin. "I have just never heard them used for naming actual businesses."

"What are the names of places on your side?" I asked.

"Well, most don't have a name, per se, they are owned and known by their wares. Some names are more famous than others, but nothing as colorful as it is here."

"They're lame," I said, grumbling. His side sounded much cooler than Rice Rice Baby, which was one local Chinese takeout.

"They can't walk?" he asked after a second.

"Lame," I repeated, and realized that wasn't going to help. "Um... stupid. Not cool. No, that probably doesn't work either. Not popular?"

He shook his head, and I tried not to get lost in the way weak sunlight playing across his hair turned its color to something I'd never seen before. "Your side uses a fair number of idioms. It makes translation difficult at best. I've understood the instructors well enough at your academy, but the other students seemed to be speaking another language altogether."

"We do have our slang," I admitted. "Why would you end up

going to high school anyways? There has to be a better place to learn about our side."

"Well, this was the closest learning establishment from the facilitation point. I figured since the students looked roughly my age it would be easier to mask my presence and learn what I could."

"And what have you learned?" I asked as we stood in line for tickets.

"That your world is nothing like mine," he shared in a whisper.

That much I agreed with.

I paid for our tickets, and I saw Hawk watching the money I handed over. As we walked into the lobby I offered him a dollar bill to examine. He scrutinized the piece of paper closely, turning it over and over again as if he was memorizing it. "You hungry?" I asked as he was on his third pass of the bill. He looked up quickly and nodded. "Famished," he answered. I steered him into line at the concession stand as he continued his inspection.

I was about to ask him what he was doing when the sound of Pink's "F**kin' Perfect" came drifting from my pocket. I barely noticed the way Hawk seemed to stiffen up at the sound because I knew that was Jewel's ring tone. "I have to take this," I said to him, as I flipped my cell open.

"Hey," I said, wondering if we were still fighting.

"Okay. So we both suck, so can we move past it?" she asked without any preamble.

I felt a weight come off my chest. "I am so down with that."

I heard her laugh. "Awesome. So, no school! What are we going to do?" she asked.

I looked over at Hawk who was watching me intently while I talked into the cell. He was clearly studying the device, as if he was trying to figure out how it worked, what it did, if it was dangerous.

"Um. Something came up. Can we do something maybe later or tomorrow?" There was no way I could explain Hawk's innate oddness without revealing he was from another world.

"Oh," she said, trying to cover her disappointment. "Something bad?"

"Um… not bad, but I just need to take care of something." I felt shitty for lying, but I couldn't see any other way out.

"Okay, well give me a call when you're free," she said, sounding hopeful I would.

"I will, promise," I said, hanging up. "Sorry," I said to Hawk, tucking the phone away.

"That's a tellyphone?" he asked in wonderment.

I forced myself not to laugh at the word. "Telephone," I corrected him. "Yeah it's called a cell."

"As in prison?"

It took me a second to connect cell phone to a cell in a prison. "Same word, different meaning."

He rolled his eyes as he went back to the dollar. "So this is currency for your realm?" I nodded. "And this man was a leader?" he asked, pointing the image of George Washington. Another nod. "He is a powerfully ugly man. He had to have seized power by some fortuitous means."

Now I did burst out laughing since I always thought Washington was pretty ugly too. "He was a general," I said, exhausting my knowledge of our first president in one sentence.

He handed the dollar back to me. "It seems a pretty flimsy means of currency. Vulnerable to flame, water, and easily torn." It was obvious he did not think much of our money.

I shoved it in my pocket as I asked, "So what do you guys use?"

"Gold or gems preferably," he answered as he looked at the menu for the concession stand. "What's a Coke?"

"Sweet drink with carbonation," I answered quickly. "Gold? Like solid gold?" I asked, amazed.

He nodded as we moved up closer to the counter. "Well, it's mixed with small quantities of other metals to help strengthen it because gold is a soft metal, but it's mostly gold, yes. Why does the corn pop?" he asked, looking back to me.

"Um, oil and something inside I think," I said, trying to wrap my mind around the idea of having actual gold coins in my pocket. "How much does stuff cost in your world anyways?"

He shrugged as he peered into the candy case. "I don't know. The royal family doesn't pay for anything. Is that an actual finger of butter?"

I looked at the cashier. "One Coke, one bottled water, large popcorn, extra butter, and two hot dogs."

His face paled. "They aren't made of real dogs, are they?"

The look on his face made it impossible for me not to laugh. "No, just meat," I assured him. "We don't eat dogs in this country."

He sighed. "But you eat fingers made out of butter?"

I looked at the cashier. "And put a Butterfinger on there too." I looked at Hawk. "You'll like it, trust me."

He didn't look convinced.

SPIKE perched on the roof of a restaurant opposite the theater and watched them through the front windows.

He had followed them at a considerable distance. Distances, however, meant nothing to a creature that could possess bird eyes along with cat ears. The boy was poisoning the prince against him, and that was not going to do. Spike had risked everything to flee with Hawk, even if the boy had no idea of the cost to him. The Changeling knew he couldn't go back to his world now, not after who he had betrayed. He'd made his choice, and at the time, he'd picked Hawk.

Yet Hawk only had eyes for the human.

He didn't like the way the human made Hawk smile. He didn't

like how close together they stood. He didn't like the way the prince's body reacted to their proximity. Hawk's pupils were larger, his heart rate was elevated, and he was giving off insane amounts of pheromones. Spike used the senses of the animals into which he could change to hear and smell and see everything as clearly as possible. Everything about Hawk told Spike that the prince was attracted to Kane.

As they walked further into the building a low growl issued from the Changeling's throat. His talons began to bore holes into the stone ledge that he was perched on as he imagined the human's neck in his grip.

KANE juggled their food as they walked into the theater. Hawk kept picking at the popcorn, enjoying the salty butter immensely. "This is incredible!" he exclaimed a bit too loudly for a theater. The movie hadn't started yet, but they still got a few glances.

In a lower voice Kane said, "I'm sure they have great food in your world too."

Hawk nodded as he grabbed another handful of popcorn and said, "Not that common people can just walk up and buy. Nothing like this!"

Kane suddenly stopped in his tracks as Hawk bumped into him. The prince looked confused as he swallowed the popcorn. "What?"

"I'm one of those common people," Kane said, his tone stern.

"I didn't mean... I meant other...," Hawk stammered.

"Is there a positive way to take being called one of the 'common people'?" Kane asked.

Hawk looked chagrined as he saw the anger in Kane's eyes. "I apologize." He added in a very low voice, "I meant no offense."

"I'm not offended," Kane clarified. "I'm more upset that you think common people are somehow worse than everyone else."

Hawk seemed to consider adding something but wisely decided to stay quiet.

Kane didn't push the point as he continued to look for a seat. He decided on three rows from the front, which should give them a buffer from the few people who were watching the movie as well. Kane handed Hawk the bottle of water and a hot dog as they settled in. He watched Hawk sniff the meat for a couple of seconds before taking a hesitant bite. He nodded to himself and then took a bigger bite and then another. Kane chuckled; Hawk obviously liked his first hot dog. "And this isn't dog, right?" he asked when he was halfway through.

Kane shrugged as he began eating his own. "I hope not."

He almost burst out laughing at the look on Hawk's face when he gave the hot dog a careful stare. The lights began to dim, and Kane settled in for the movie. "So what is this play about?" Hawk asked, still not whispering.

Kane whispered back. "It's about a guy who goes to another world and ends up falling in love with a native." He paused as he realized what had just fallen out of his mouth. "It's just what was playing!" he added quickly. "It's just a popular movie." His words sounded lame, even to himself.

Hawk gave him a wry grin as he sat back and relaxed. "Well, at least it's a believable tale."

Kane was grateful for the darkness since it hid his blushing.

CHAPTER EIGHT

THE movie was like nothing he had ever seen before.

The creatures on the screen vaguely resembled a cross between a water dweller and a werecat but were something different altogether. They communed with a great tree, which was fascinating to Hawk since he had never heard of anyone else that practiced it as well. He had been enraptured the entire time, caught up in the story as well as the majesty of the images. When the warrior's brother ended up with the girl, Hawk had found tears rolling down his cheeks, unashamed, the emotion in his heart clearly expressed on his face.

Kane had seen the movie three times already, but seeing it through Hawk's eyes changed it entirely. At one very suspenseful point during the movie, Hawk had taken Kane's hand. Kane stared at their joined hands for a good ten minutes before he was able to concentrate on the movie again. He wasn't about to let go of Hawk's hand, and as the movie wound down, he noticed that Hawk didn't make a move to release him either. At some point they made eye contact, and Hawk's smile made his heart jump a few beats. Something happened on the screen, and his head turned back like he was a ten-year-old.

Kane knew he was falling hard for this guy.

When the movie was over, Hawk sat there, skimming the credits, and when it was clear nothing else was going to be shown, he turned to Kane. "Will they play it again?"

Kane nodded. The huge smile that spread across Hawk's face was infectious. He looked around and then declared, "We will need more popped corn first!" They stood up and made their way to the lobby, still hand in hand. There were more people than the last showing, and the lobby was filling up. Kane had known they were still holding hands, but he suddenly became *aware* of the fact. And more aware that he had no desire to stop.

"Where are the facilities?" Hawk asked in a low voice.

"The bathroom?" Kane asked to clarify. He was shocked to see Hawk blush slightly at the word. Instead of answering he just nodded slightly. "Come on, that Coke went right through me." He started to walk toward the restroom when he felt Hawk's hand pull. He looked back and saw he was just standing there looking at him. "What?" he had to ask.

"You're going with me?" Hawk asked in a horrified whisper.

"I have to use it also."

"Together?" Hawk asked again, obviously far closer to aghast than to horrified.

Kane burst out laughing. "It's a public restroom. No, not together but, yes, we share the room."

Hawk didn't say anything for almost a minute before managing to stutter. "I can wait."

Kane rolled his eyes and pulled him into the bathroom, ignoring Hawk's token resistance. Thankfully, the room was empty, so Kane maneuvered Hawk toward an open stall. "You use that, I'll be out here."

Hawk looked at him skeptically as he slowly closed the door. Kane moved to the nearest urinal and began to unzip his pants. Hawk's voice sounded distressed when he called, "Um… what is this thing?"

Kane stopped and zipped his pants back up. "What's wrong?"

"There's water in here," Hawk's voice replied.

"It's a toilet," Kane said, not understanding the statement.

"Yes, but there is water in here. How does it work?"

Kane tried not to sigh as he leaned up against the stall. "I don't understand," he asked. "Haven't you used the bathroom since you've been here?"

"I voided my bowels, yes," he said, sounding embarrassed. "The house has a large back area."

Kane remembered why he had hated going to the Renaissance Fair: no indoor plumbing.

"Ruber, please tell me you can explain a toilet to him? I have a feeling if I do he might have a stroke," Kane asked hopefully.

"Of course. I live to serve," the ruby answered in an acidic tone.

"I'm going to wait outside!" Kane called out.

"Please leave!" The panic in Hawk's voice almost brought Kane to a halt; Hawk sounded really frightened. However, Ruber bobbed up over the top of the stall and shooed Kane away by making the gem lord's equivalent of a pushing motion.

Kane went and stood guard outside the restroom.

SPIKE saw the human come out of the room, and he couldn't control the snarling growl that coiled from his chest.

The boy was smiling as if sharing a private joke with himself, and it infuriated him because he was sure the joke involved Hawk.

Spike had considered attempting the shift into human form so he could enter the building, but that was taking a greater risk than he was willing to make. His kind had the ability to assume various forms, but most of them came from mimicking smaller creatures from the animal kingdom. The subtleties of maintaining a human face while coordinating bipedal movement for long periods of time were draining enough to cause permanent damage to his shape-changing abilities.

But the thought was tempting.

He was wavering between two possibilities: letting caution fly to the wind and shifting into human form and walking into the theater to

79

at the very least hear what they were talking about, or heading to the human's house and destroying everything he treasured. Then he considered first destroying the house and then coming back to attack the boy, but he wasn't sure how to distract the prince. Spike mulled all his possibilities to the point that he almost missed the plump girl walking by the front of the theater.

She would have been utterly forgettable to him if she hadn't stopped in her tracks and openly gaped at the human standing by the door through which Hawk had gone. Spike checked twice to make sure they were looking at the same human. He could hear her mutter under her breath, "Taking care of something, my ass." The Changeling wasn't sure what her words meant, but he was paying rapt attention. She continued to stare, mumbling about "how could he lie to her like that" when Hawk walked out to join the boy.

"Oh that makes perfect sense," she said a little more loudly, her voice obviously upset.

Spike began to understand. The girl had feelings for the human like he had for the prince. He wondered if she wanted to kill the human as much as he did? She stomped off, her fists clenched in rage.

Spike watched her take off and then turned his attention back to Hawk and his pet human.

HE CAME out of the bathroom looking three different kinds of embarrassed. He was so adorable I could have puked.

"So, everything okay?" I asked as diplomatically as I could.

He nodded almost imperceptibly, and now three kinds of embarrassment became four kinds of embarrassment. "Thank you," he mumbled.

"I'll be right back," I said, quickly rushing past him into the bathroom.

HAWK waited for Kane to finish as he wandered around the lobby.

Though none of the people walking through were as attractive as the people in Arcadia, he could appreciate the quaintness of their way of life. It reminded him of the One World celebration, when people from every world made a pilgrimage to Arcadia to give thanks for the world's continued existence. Dwarfs from

Djupur, a few strays from Aponiviso, and of course, a variety of others from all over. Hawk felt an ache of homesickness constrict his heart.

So far, he had tried not thinking about the fate of his parents, if they were even still alive, but the movie had opened a box of emotions in his heart that he was finding hard to close again. A small child stood at the counter buying what Kane had called "candy" with its mother, and that was the last straw. He felt his eyes begin to tear up, and he looked away quickly.

When Kane came out, he found the prince in the corner, trying to fight back his tears.

"What's wrong?" Kane asked in a worried tone.

Hawk's voice cracked as he choked out, "I want to go home."

Without a thought, Kane just wrapped his arms around Hawk and held him as he cried.

I DIDN'T know why he was crying, but I could almost feel his pain.

He was fighting the emotion as best he could, but all that seemed to do was make it worse. I couldn't imagine being stranded on another world, away from my dad and Jewel, all alone with no idea how I was going to get back. I knew for a fact it would suck in a very real way. He buried his face in my shirt as I moved him further back, away from the rest of the lobby. It was half not wanting to embarrass him more by having strangers see him break down and half I wasn't sure I wanted people to see me hugging a guy.

Which was confusing as hell to me.

"Hey," I said, trying to calm him down. "It's okay. You'll get home."

"You don't know that," he said, his eyes red with tears.

It was true, I didn't know that at all. But I wasn't just saying it to make him feel better, I didn't think for a second he wasn't going to get back. "No, I don't, but I am willing to bet if there is something you truly want, there isn't anything in the world... well, worlds, that can stop you."

He wiped his eyes as he searched my face for sincerity. "You mean that?"

"You have the earring on," I said with a grin. "You know I do."

He smiled back, and it was like the sun coming out after a storm. "So when does the next play unthaw?"

I shook my head as I chuckled. "The next showing starts in like ten minutes," I said.

"Excellent!" he said, standing up straighter. "I cannot wait to see what happens to the Jake and Neytiri."

I paused. "Um, you do know it is the same story right?"

He nodded quickly. "Yes, I wish to know what happens next in the story."

"Um... it's just the same movie again," I tried to explain. He just stared at me, obviously not getting it. "It is the same thing we just saw, not the next part. They have to go and make a sequel, and that will take years." Another blank stare. "They have to build sets and write the script...."

He finally sighed and handed me the earring.

I repeated myself, and I would have killed to know how the magic earring translated the process of making a movie to him, but he nodded as if understanding. "Well then, that's less exciting," he said when I was done.

"We can go get actual food," I offered.

He gave me a wary look. "The food we just ate wasn't real?"

I let out a quick bark of laughter as I saw him get scared about the hot dog again.

"It was food, but I mean... oh come on!" I said, grabbing his arm and leading him outside.

"Just tell me it wasn't really dog," he said as we walked out the door.

HAWK was pleasantly surprised by the little tavern Kane took him to.

He didn't see any place for rooms, but the smell of food in the small area was almost intoxicating. There didn't seem to be many people present, and the serving girl had far too many clothes on, but it didn't matter much to him. Kane picked up some kind of hardened paper and was browsing it when the woman put down a glass with water and ice. Hawk marveled at the condensation on the tumbler as he held it up. "Actual ice?" he commented. "This must be an expensive eatery."

The waitress looked at Hawk and then to Kane. "Your friend French?" she asked.

Kane didn't understand the question until he realized that Hawk wasn't wearing the earring. "Um... yeah," Kane answered slowly. "He's an exchange student."

"I'm a what?" Hawk asked in mid-sip.

"Oh, well, they grow 'em handsome in France," she said with a wink. "What are you boys having?"

"What are you hungry for?" Kane asked Hawk and then instantly regretted it.

"He understands English?" she asked, embarrassed. Turning to him she asked, "What would you like?"

Hawk looked at her blankly and asked Kane, "Is she talking to me?"

"Oh, I forgot!" Kane said like an idiot. "How about we split a rosemary chicken with the baby potatoes."

"Your potatoes have children?" Hawk asked paling. "And you eat them?"

Kane ignored him as he handed the menus to the woman. "And maybe some bread?"

She nodded and smiled at Hawk. Before she walked away she commented, "He sure does seem to understand you."

I shrugged, laughing, wishing she'd hurry and get out of earshot.

"You forgot the earring again," I said, once she was gone.

He nodded. "I figured that out when she talked." He held his hand out. "Pass it back."

"I can't!" I whispered, as she looked across the restaurant at us. "I told her you weren't from here and didn't speak English. If you suddenly start making sense, she'll get suspicious."

"Fair point," Hawk said, pulling his hand back. "Well then, you are going to have to translate for me."

Kane nodded as he took a sip of water, wondering how people lied all the time without losing their mind. "So you were asking about the ice?"

The prince's attention went back to the glass. "How expensive is the ice water? I can't imagine it is cheap."

"It's free," Kane said, confused.

Hawk began to choke on his water. "What? How is that possible?"

"Um, ice machine?" he explained.

"A machine that makes ice? Honestly?" he marveled. "How does it work?"

Kane opened his mouth and then closed it. "I have no idea to be honest. I know you put water in and it freezes it."

"I've seen ice magic practiced in a few realms, but I've never heard of a machine that could harness it. You could become rich selling its secret to Shahryar and his kind."

"Who?" Kane asked.

"King of kings for the desert lands in the Masaut'wa," Hawk explained, looking around for food.

"Yeah, I bet an ice machine would rock in the desert." The waitress started walking over with a tray of bread and Kane said, "She's coming over, shhhh!"

"Why?" Hawk said with an evil grin. "She can't understand me."

Kane started to protest but had to just smile at her as she put the warm loaf down. "Fresh from the oven," she said, smiling.

"It smells almost as delicious as you," Hawk said, enjoying the way Kane tried not to react to the words.

"He says thank you."

"No, I said there are better things to put butter on and to lick it off than bread."

Kane's face froze as he smiled at her. "And that it smells delicious."

She turned to Hawk. "Well thank you," she said slowly.

"Ask her if there is a room open with a strong bed," Hawk teased as he nodded at her.

"We're good," Kane said quickly to her.

"Okay, your food's almost done."

"You're more than good," Hawk said seductively.

She laughed as she walked away. "Tell him that French sounds so sexy!"

"You're a jerk!" Kane hissed once she was across the room.

Hawk tore off a piece of the bread and laughed. "And you are insanely attractive when you're mad."

Kane said nothing as he stuffed some bread in his mouth.

ATHENS didn't have a homeless population as much as it had a group of individuals that preferred to live outside.

There were more than a few folk who called People's Park home, and they didn't seem to mind at all. A couple of businesses collected leftovers for them and Beyond Bed and Bath, the local home furnishing store, always seemed to have a couple of blankets around when it got colder. There was a homeless shelter in town, but it was rarely used unless the weather got too severe; in Athens, being homeless just didn't carry the same stigma it did in larger towns. Most were men, former veterans, who had never found their way back from war but who had been able to come as far as the friendly town. They called it home and, for a lot of them, the war receded a little farther back into their memories.

No one was crass enough to refer to the men as mentally unstable, but there were a couple who were provided regular meds when their assigned social workers made the rounds. One such man was Robin Famis, an older man who usually wandered around town with an old camping lantern in hand claiming he was different famous people depending on his mood. Most of the time he was harmless and easily redirected back to the park by people who found him far from "home." People's Park was where he seemed to be most comfortable. He was usually accompanied by a stray dog that had adopted him one summer. Robin had famously named him Dog.

It wasn't odd to see Robin and Dog walking the street at night, the man offering his long-dead lantern in case someone needed light and Dog offering his invaluable presence as a cute dog, willing to eat any stray food looking for a stomach to stay. They were staples of life in Athens, and no one paid them any mind at all. With the weather growing colder and colder, Robin knew he was going to have to take to sleeping in the shelter soon, which depressed him. The staff there never needed his lantern for light and wouldn't allow Dog to sleep with him since he wasn't allowed in the building. But a warm bed was better than freezing to death in the park, and they always put something out for Dog in the back alley.

Besides, no matter how cold it got, the weather always got warmer after a while.

The two of them were working their way toward the shelter, since it looked like it might rain. Robin would have liked to have been out in the rain, in case someone needed his light, but as he grew older, he found the dampness simply too much to bear. If Dog had had hands he could have taught him how to use the lantern, but alas, the dog refused to grow thumbs, and Robin seemed unable to get younger. So it was off to the shelter for both of them.

They were mere blocks from the shelter when Dog began to growl.

It was a new sound for the dog, and Robin frankly had no idea he could make it. He knew rationally that Dog was a dog but his companion was normally so friendly that the idea of him being anything else slipped his mind. However, it was obvious that Dog was, in fact, a dog and was upset at something in the alley between Glen's Restaurant (which was a pun because it was in fact Gloria's restaurant) and Gloria's Herb shack (which was of course owned and run by Glen).

"What is it, boy?" Robin asked, wishing for the umpteenth time that Dog would hurry up and learn to speak English already.

The dog barked once, his legs set, as he stared into the darkness of the alley.

Robin held his lantern up, hoping it might shed some light onto the cause of his friend's discomfort.

Which was the last thing Robin would remember.

GLORIA brought us our food, and I saw Hawk's attention turn from teasing me to the roasted chicken in her hands. Even though we had gorged ourselves on movie crap I was suddenly starving looking at the food in front of us. "You guys good?" she asked, seeing us both ready to gnaw our own hands off from hunger.

"This looks incredible," I told her as Hawk took one of the plates and started to cut a leg off the chicken.

"Well, try not to eat so fast you don't enjoy it," she commented as she watched Hawk devour the meat off the bone in one large gulp.

I kicked his shin as she walked away. "I thought royalty was supposed to have manners!" I chastised him.

"I'm hungry!" he said with his mouth full.

I rolled my eyes and served some of the chicken to myself. As usual, it was awesome. Gloria's was the best non-weird restaurant in town, her only claim to fame was everything she served was organically grown and raised. From the chicken and the wheat for the bread to the herbs and the apple tart for dessert, everything had reached our table free of chemicals. You wouldn't think it would make that big a difference, but trust me, it does.

I wasn't sure how they made food on Hawk's world, but he seemed to like the chicken just fine. We both shoveled food into our mouths, all thought of conversation put on hold until our stomachs were full. I heard the front door open but we ignored it since it wasn't between the food and our mouths.

We didn't pay it any attention until the screaming started.

GLORIA served the two boys and couldn't stop smiling.

She was pretty sure that the two of them didn't think it looked like they were on a date, but it was pretty obvious that the two of them were head over heels about each other. She knew Kane's dad pretty well, and he had commented more than once that his son was miserable being the only gay teenager in town, so seeing him smiling with someone else was a good thing.

She was about to grab the pitcher to refill their water when the front door opened.

Gloria turned and saw Robin walk into the restaurant, he looked lost. She normally set aside some food for him and Dog, but he'd never come inside to retrieve them. Most of the time, she left them out back for them because Robin was notoriously touchy about handouts. He was a proud man, and in the summer, he'd insist on cleaning her windows or washing the back alley in compensation. Gloria was happy to give him these little jobs since it allowed the man some dignity, so him actually walking in was new.

"Hi, Robin," she said, walking up to him. She could hear Dog barking outside, and the canine did not sound happy. "Everything okay?" He didn't say anything as he looked around the dining room, his eyes focusing on the two boys instantly. Gloria began to worry about the look on the man's face and took another step toward him. Seeing him coming through the front door and looking lost struck a warning note in the back of her mind. "Robin, are you hungry?"

He turned toward her, and his hand swung her way.

She screamed as his knife sliced across her chest. Gloria tumbled backward, and she collided with the table behind her and went falling to the side in shock. There was the sound of breaking glass from behind the counter as the other woman on duty dropped her tray and screamed at the sight of a man wielding a bloody knife in the doorway.

Both Hawk and Kane turned as one.

"Get down," Hawk said to Kane, kicking his chair back as he summoned Truheart to his hand.

Kane looked at the sword, to Robin, and then back to the sword. "No!" he cried out. "You can't hurt him. He's sick!"

Robin turned, orientating himself toward Hawk instantly. He began to lumber toward them, his mouth pulled back into a grin.

His teeth were a dark blue.

"Berserker weed!" Hawk called out as he moved around the table toward him.

Kane grabbed his arm and tried to restrain him. "He's just a homeless guy! He's not a danger."

Hawk shrugged the hand off of him as he glared at the man. "Kane, back away. This man's been enspelled, he is not in his right mind."

Kane moved in front of Hawk. "That's what I'm saying. You can't hurt him."

Hawk looked past him and focused on Robin and his knife. "Get out of my way."

Kane's features hardened as he refused to move. "I'm not letting you hurt—" And then he let out a scream. Hawk caught him as he fell forward. Robin had moved faster than Hawk was prepared for and plunged the knife into the small of the boy's back. Hawk twisted, lowering the body to the ground with his hands and kicking the man in the stomach with his foot.

Robin staggered back a few steps, but it was obvious the blow had done no real damage to him. Hawk let Kane go as he said in a low voice, "Ruber, attend to his wounds."

When Hawk turned back to the man, he was a little shocked to find the bearded face right next to his. He saw the steak knife move at his gut and reacted instantly. Truheart barely blocked the blade, forcing Hawk to take a few steps back. As soon as he did, the man moved to stab the prone body of Kane on the floor. The knife descended toward the boy's neck when Ruber faded into visibility.

The knife shattered against the enchanted stone, shards of the metal embedding into Robin's face and neck. "I don't think so," Ruber pronounced as it ignored the combat and began to concentrate on Kane's wound. Hawk took advantage of the man's hesitation and lunged over Kane to attack. It was obvious the man was dosed on berserker weed by the stains on his teeth and the way he was seemingly impervious to pain. A magical herb that was found only in the deepest depths of The Lost Jungle, it made normal men virtually unstoppable juggernauts in battle for little more than an hour. Once given a target, they were one-man armies that could withstand the greatest of wounds until the herb wore off.

And then the enchantment killed them.

Hawk saw the man grab another knife off a table and move forward at him again. He had no doubt he could stop the crazed maniac, but if Kane's cries were true then this was just an innocent person that the Dark had used to get to him. He focused on Truheart as he began to circle around the man, drawing his attention away from Kane and Ruber. He was worried about Kane, but he didn't have any concentration to spare as he began to recite his magic silently.

The blade began to change from its normal metal hue to the blue, indicating that magic was in play. Hawk dodged the man's lunging swing easily, even though it was far faster than a normal human's speed. The herb's enchantment was burning through Robin's system at an alarming rate. The sword began to openly glow now, the blue brightening more and more until it was surrounded by a white nimbus of energy. The prince hoped Kane was right about the man as he waited for the man to attack again before moving.

Uttering an arcane word, he shoved the sword into the man's chest up to the hilt.

There was a blinding flash of light as Truheart dispelled the enchanted herb's magic, cleansing the man's body instantly. Both combatants were locked together for a moment as the magic drained from the human and into the sword. Hawk saw the man's eyes come slightly back to focus as he looked at him. Robin still seemed dazed as he uttered, "Must… kill… Kane…."

Hawk froze in shock for a moment. "What did you say?"

Blood suddenly burst onto his face as the man's chest seemingly exploded. Hawk automatically took three steps back as the man collapsed to the ground, revealing Spike behind him, one talon covered in blood. He looked at Hawk with a smile. "I saved you."

CHAPTER NINE

"WHAT did you do?" Hawk said, his face white with shock.

Spike's smile fell instantly. "He was attacking you...," he began to say.

The fury on Hawk's face silenced the Changeling before it could say another word. "Ruber," he called over his shoulder. "Is Kane okay?"

"The wound is healed, but he is still in shock," the ruby answered.

"See to the woman," he ordered, his eyes never leaving Spike's. Without a word, the gem flew over to where Gloria had passed out and began to bathe her with a kaleidoscope of red beams. "You were ordered to stay at the house," he said to Spike in a low voice.

"I am charged with your protection...," he started to explain.

"You're charged to follow my orders!"

Hawk's explosion froze everyone in the restaurant in their place. Even Ruber paused for a moment before going back to tend to Gloria's stab wound. In a more controlled voice, the prince added, "It was after Kane, not me."

Spike's eyes grew wide in surprise. "The Dark sent an assassin after the boy? Sire, he is in great danger."

Hawk blinked a few times before he looked away from the shape shifter's golden eyes. He rubbed his head as he mumbled. "It was the Dark... they are trying to hurt me through the boy."

Spike moved closer to him. "We are endangering the boy by just being here," he whispered.

"We are putting him in danger," Hawk repeated, still not looking up.

"*You* are putting him in danger," Spike clarified.

Hawk's head shot up as he exclaimed, "I'm putting the boy in danger!" He turned to see the still unconscious form of Kane on the floor, and his heart was flooded with guilt. "We need to get away from here, before they harm anyone else." Hawk turned his face away from Kane only to see the cook and the other waitress looking at them in utter and complete shock. "They've seen too much. Charm their memories while I attend to the boy."

Spike's smile returned. "As you command." And he bounded across the room to land on the counter in one move.

Hawk knelt down next to Kane, resting his hand on the other boy's cheek for a moment. "I'm sorry," he said.

Kane's eyes fluttered open weakly. "For what?" he asked.

Hawk's smile was bittersweet as he explained, "I am endangering you. I have to go."

Kane tried to sit up and winced as he fell back with a gasp. "Oh God!" he cried out suddenly.

"See? Stay still, you'll be fine once I'm gone."

Kane grabbed Hawk's hand and held it tight. "I will be anything but fine if you leave."

Hawk squeezed the hand back and then slowly removed his own from the grip. "Possibly. But you'll be alive." He leaned down and kissed him on the forehead and whispered, "I'm so sorry."

Kane tried to hold on to him as he stood, but didn't have the strength. "Please don't...." he begged, but fell back onto the ground as his back began to throb.

Hawk walked over to where Ruber floated above the woman and knelt down. "She's alive?" he asked.

"Alive and well," Ruber answered. "This was not your fault."

Hawk looked at the dead man and shook his head. "This is very much my fault. What will happen if no one remembers the event? And they find the man dead and the two of them wounded?"

Ruber considered it for a few moments. "Well, it would be unusual, but they would suspect the man burst in and attacked them for lack of any other logical explanation."

"Excellent. You belong to Kane now. Your job is to protect and keep him safe." He looked at the gem. "You understand, correct?"

Ruber bobbed in the air in lieu of a nod. "I do, your highness, but things are not as they…."

"It's done," Spike said, leaping back to Hawk's side. "They sleep now but will not remember you nor the attack."

"Good work," Hawk said, standing. "We need to go. Ruber, you have your orders."

"Sire, if you will listen for a moment…," the ruby started to say.

"We are leaving, gemling." Spike hissed angrily. "You can't stop that."

Ruber's glow intensified for a moment before Hawk put a hand on Spike's shoulder. "He's right, Ruber. We have to go. Stay with Kane."

"Of course, sir but…," Ruber tried again.

"We'll use the back exit, Spike," Hawk said, ignoring the words. "And go back to the house."

"I'll cover our rear," it said, as Hawk began to walk out, refusing to look back.

Spike glanced at Kane and Ruber and smiled as they left them behind.

WHEN I woke up he was gone.

The police were covering Robin's body with a sheet as the paramedics checked Gloria's wounds. It took me a few seconds to realize that no one was paying any attention to me. "Ruber?" I asked quietly.

His voice came from just over my shoulder. "We are invisible," he explained. "I thought it best to remove ourselves from the situation."

I watched them load Gloria onto their paramedic gurney and push her out to the ambulance. "Is she okay?" I asked.

"She will be," Ruber assured me.

"Good." I tried to get up and felt a pain shoot up my back. "Oh crap!" I cried out loudly. I froze as I saw the two cops look over to where Ruber was hiding me.

"Time to leave?" Ruber asked as they began to thread their way among tables toward us.

"Definitely."

"Close your eyes," Ruber warned as he flared into visibility and instantly flooded the room with a blinding light. I had covered my eyes and still I saw spots as I struggled to see again. "Keep your eyes shut." I heard Ruber say, this time much closer to me than before. I clenched them shut as a strange whine filled the area. It felt as if we were in a wind tunnel all of a sudden as a gust of air hit my face and almost blew me back onto the floor.

My ears popped and then I heard nothing.

I'm not sure how much time passed, but the next thing I knew, I felt myself fall maybe half an inch onto my ass. "You can open them now," Ruber advised in a calm voice.

I cracked one eye open and was shocked to find myself sitting on my living room floor.

I tried to get up again but the pain was too much for me to manage. I collapsed onto my back and stared at the ceiling in pain, despairing. "How long am I going to be like this?"

"You were stabbed through your lower back less than thirty minutes ago. Assume that you will need more time than that to recover," Ruber said, as he floated into my line of sight.

"How long before I can stand again?" I snapped, trying to not shout at him.

"The spell will require another thirty minutes before it heals you completely."

I sighed and laid my head down and tried not to think about how Hawk had left me.

THEY made good time back to the house.

Hawk didn't feel anything magical or evil around him, but then, the entire point of being an assassin was not to be noticed. Spike trailed him in the trees by about half a block, hiding himself to make sure they weren't being followed. If the Dark could find the two of them in a restaurant, it would take nothing to track them back to the house. His mind raced, wondering if Kane was okay and if Ruber was able to defend him, but he forced the thoughts away as he focused on what was in front of him. He paused at the front door as he waited for Spike to leap from the treetop across to the second floor of the house. He counted to ten in his mind and then charged into the house.

Nothing.

The house was exactly as he had left it earlier; there was no sign of anything that spelled danger. Spike came down the stairs, nodding to Hawk, indicating that the upstairs was safe as well. "We are alone."

Hawk walked around the room, gathering his belongings and tossing them into his pack. "We are leaving," he said, as the magic of the bag absorbed more and more. "When is the next time we can cross over?"

Spike was picking up things as well, making a pile of clothes and equipment next to Hawk's bedroll. "Not until sunrise," the Changeling answered after a moment's thought. "Only in the blue hour is the wall thin enough."

Hawk nodded as he threw the last of his gear in and fastened the top. "Then we wait until morning," he said, sitting in the chair, Truheart in hand.

"I will stand watch," Spike said, coming closer. "You should rest up before we leave."

Hawk shook his head. "I'm fine. The assassins can come at any moment."

"We're safe for now," Spike countered, his voice becoming deeper. "And you are so tired."

Hawk let out a huge yawn in response. "I am tired."

"You're safe for now. I will stand watch," Spike said in a softer voice.

"… safe." Hawk repeated, his eyes closing slowly.

"And you don't care for the boy," Spike said, his voice almost a whisper.

"No," Hawk said, his eyes opening wide. "I do care! He's in danger!" He started to rise groggily. Spike began talking quickly, his voice taking on the same husky tone he had started with.

"The boy is safe, we are safe. You're tired… you're just so tired."

Hawk fell back into the chair, his eyes heavy again as he repeated, "So tired…."

"You'd be more comfortable sleeping without your shirt, wouldn't you?" Spike suggested.

As if in a dream, Hawk pulled off his shirt and tossed it to the floor.

"You're safe," Spike said as the prince fell asleep. "And the boy is too," he said more to himself as he picked up the shirt. Without making a sound, he slipped on the shirt and began pulling a pair of jeans out of the pack. "But not for long."

TRUE to Ruber's estimate, forty minutes passed before I could stand up. Well, in a manner of speaking, I could stand.

What had been a mortal wound had been reduced first to an agonizing pain and finally just a sore back. I raised my hands over my head and stretched, and instantly regretted it. "Okay, that hurt," I said, sitting gingerly down in my dad's chair.

"May I suggest not doing that then?" Ruber said, oh so helpfully.

I think I might have grunted a response, but honestly, I was too tired and too depressed to care. He'd left me. He had kissed my forehead and left me, and I didn't know how to feel about that. I mean sure, I was pissed, but that was the easy reaction. I knew he was leaving for my own good, and that made me mad because I wasn't some lame-ass Disney princess waiting for my prince to come.

Even though he was like an actual prince and all, and how freaking cool was that?

I was worried about him; he was in danger, and I wanted to help him. How? Well, that part was fuzzy, but I knew I had to help him. He was… he was inside of me somehow, and I knew I was inside of him. There was something pulling us together, and I didn't care anymore if I was in danger. Danger didn't matter if I was with him.

Oh God, I sounded like a Disney princess.

"Ruber, how much trouble is he in?" I asked, trying to summon the strength to stand.

"Far more than he knows," the gem answered, floating back toward me. "He is under the belief he is under attack by the Dark when that is not the source of the conflict."

I understood maybe half of that. "Say again?"

"He believes the attacker in the restaurant…."

"Robin."

He seemed a bit perturbed by the interruption but acknowledged the man had a name. "...he believes that Robin was enchanted by beserker weed and sent to attack you by the Dark."

That made more sense. "Then who did?"

Before he could answer there was a knock on the door. "Hide yourself," I said to him, in case it was an actual human who didn't know things like floating British-speaking gems existed. I limped over to the door. The pain had mellowed to a manageable dull ache. I opened the door and tried not to react to Hawk standing there.

"Can I come in?" he asked.

I stepped back and allowed Hawk to enter.

"You came back," I said, shocked. I honestly thought he had left for good.

"Of course I came back. You have to know how I feel about you," Hawk said, turning back to me and smiling.

I froze in place as a different set of words spoke over his voice. *"Of course I came back to kill you."*

"What?" I asked, my mouth growing dry.

His smile was devastating, his eyes were alive with emotion, but there was something missing as he looked at me. I no longer felt the warmth, the connection I normally sensed being this close to him; instead it seemed to me he was almost... hungry? "I can't keep this up," he said, taking a step toward me. The words were the same, but this time the tone of his voice was angry, seething, and not with want. He reached up to stroke my cheek, and I felt myself flinch back. "I just have to have you."

"I just have to kill you."

I edged away from his hand and ducked around him, back-stepping into the living room. "Are you okay?" I asked hesitantly. "You don't seem to be yourself," I added, wondering how far I could make it toward the stairs before he reached me.

"Who else would I be?" he asked, trying to close the distance between us.

"There is no way you could know who I really am."

Now I had passed scared and found myself quickly moving into terrified.

"Um, I'm not feeling really well," I managed, putting the coffee table between him and me. "Maybe we can do this tomorrow?"

"But I need to talk to you now," he said, rounding the table.

"You need to be dead before he wakes up."

"Spike!" I exclaimed realizing what the two different voices were.

Hawk's face distorted, shifting into something alien. The only thing I saw, however, was its expression of inhuman anger. Spike's body shrank and thinned, his skin morphing into a jaundiced-yellow hide. He sprang across the table at me, Hawk's clothes falling off as he leapt. His hands elongated into what looked all too much like razor sharp talons as he flew.

I stood, frozen, stunned at the transformation. Something inside my head screamed *"Move, move, move!"* And I did.

My impulse was to jerk back, but the couch blocked me. The edge of it hit my knees, and I crumpled and flopped backward like some lame *Matrix* move. Our old couch saved my life. Spike's jump took him well over my new position, and he collided with the wall, his head crashing into the sheetrock. I rolled to the floor, pushing the coffee table over as I scrabbled toward the door. That same "Move, move, *move"* pounded through my head. The Changeling pulled its head out of the hole it had made, plaster dust falling off his face as he glared at me.

"I will end you!" he vowed. This time his words matched his intention exactly.

I tried to scramble to my feet, but I felt like I was stuck in that fucking dream where you are running and running yet getting nowhere.

The rug bunched up under me, and I fell to my hands and knees, my forward momentum destroyed. I turned over, not wanting to have this thing plunge its claws into my back. Instead, I evidently preferred watching him slice me up.

Sure enough, Spike leapt off the couch and landed on the coffee table before he came at me, arms outward, claws spread, his oversized mouth turned into a horrifying grimace complete with fangs. In less than a second, the image of Jewel slapping my head and being thrown back flashed in front of my eyes, and I called out. "*Ruber, help!*"

"Protection," the ruby announced casually, and Spike stopped falling. Instead, startled and furious, it floated a foot above me.

I saw a shimmer in the air between us, the same way that air moves above a flame. Spike's mouth returned to something normal as he began to mumble under his breath. The words vanished from my memory the instant they were spoken. What I had heard made no sense at all, which meant they had to be magic. "What's he doing?" I asked, too terrified to move.

"Dispelling the barrier," Ruber answered dispassionately.

"Stop him!" I called out.

"I am unable to harm him. He is on the list of entities I am not allowed to take offensive actions toward."

I forced myself not to curse at the rock and instead just screamed, "*Do something!*"

The ruby began to pulse with light and floated off the ground about two feet, spinning slowly at first and then faster. Ruber began to speak, in the same fleeting language Spike had used, Ruber recited something and then promptly vanished.

"What the—?" I grunted as the barrier the elemental had created disintegrated, and Spike plummeted out of the air.

Spike crashed down on top of me, slamming into me so hard I felt the breath fly out of me. I cringed when my ribs and aching back complained about the weight of his body and the force of his impact.

Spike seemed as surprised as I was and scrambled to get off of me. I didn't know a thing about Changelings. Spike was my first experience with the race, and I had to admit, so far, I was not a fan. In my complete and absolute terror, every single scrap of information I had ever heard about monsters and things that go bump in the night flashed before my eyes; the memory of one of my dad's old movies came rushing up through the haze of fear.

"Wolfmen have nads." Those three words came through clear as a bell.

My knee came up and slammed between Spike's legs. I saw his eyes bulge outward as he stopped moving and breathing. He toppled over to the left as I rolled out from under him. I still couldn't draw a full breath and clutched my chest as I staggered drunkenly to my feet. My back was on fire as whatever pain I'd moved past came flaring back a thousand fold. Spike rocked back and forth, curled in a fetal position, something like a whistling moan leaving his mouth on every breath.

I leaned against my dad's chair and tried to get my lungs to start working again before he got up.

He recovered faster than I did.

Using his index claw as a grappling hook, he punched the tip through the wallboard above him and pulled himself to his feet. If I thought he hated me before, I'd been wrong. His previous emotion had only been slight dislike compared to what he felt right now. "I was just going to kill you," he said, taking a halting step at me. "You got between him and me, and that isn't allowed. But it was nothing personal then," he wheezed at me. He dislocated his jaw and opened his mouth to roar at me, and I saw that there were more teeth in his mouth than I'd seen in a dozen people. "*Now* it's personal."

I shoved the chair between him and me. All I could do was draw maybe a quarter breath before my diaphragm threatened to knot up, cramping.

He crouched down. Still winded and hurting from my shot to his nads, he readied himself to spring. I felt the chill go down my spine as I realized I was about to die.

I squeezed my eyes shut and wished I had had time to say good-bye to my dad.

Suddenly, a flash of light pulsed against my eyelids. I opened them quickly, wondering if I was already dead. Were these the last confused thoughts shooting through my brain while I bled out on the floor? Had I seen a flash of lightning from outside?

Hawk stood between Spike and me, with Ruber floating off his right shoulder. He was wearing only his jeans and had his sword gripped in his right hand.

They glared at each other for a moment as time slowed between them.

Then they both roared and charged at each other.

HAWK was sleeping deeply when he sensed the magic change in the room.

Waking, especially since he had no memory of falling asleep, was disorienting. He went from leaning back, deep in slumber, to crouching, brandishing his sword in less than a second. He wasn't even aware what he was looking at until he felt the cold floor under his bare feet, and his mind begin to un-fog.

Then he saw that chatterbox of an elemental floating in midair and was suddenly reminded why he had avoided it with a vengeance back in Arcadia. Hawk's eyes narrowed against the bright light. "Why are you not with Ka... the human?" he asked, knowing the answer could in no way be good.

"He is under attack by your Changeling," the gem replied, its attitude subtle but very present. Hawk wondered if the jewel had resented being given as a gift yet again. He saw the pack open and clothes scattered about, and he began to piece the situation together.

Spike's jealousy had gotten the worst of him.

"Take me to them now," he commanded, stepping toward the floating artifact.

"As you wish, your *majesty*." The last word was said so scornfully Hawk knew for certain that the ruby still held a grudge. He had no time to apologize for his poor manners; that would have to wait for later. If there was a later.

He felt the wash of magics move over him as reality itself turned inside out. He closed his eyes, knowing the danger of The Nowhere that one passed through with magic. Some people, mostly Senders, loved the sight, sometimes growing addicted to the vista to the point of insanity.

He counted in his head to three and then opened them again.

Hawk had seen Spike in many different moods before. The Changeling had been his guardian since Hawk's infancy. Hawk had thought himself well versed in the shape shifter's mercurial emotions. As he stared down the murderous intent in the creature's eyes, he knew he had thought wrong.

Changelings were a rare breed, the very few ever seen at all having sworn loyalty to the royal family in one way or another. Rumors surfaced every so often of feral Changelings, posing as other animals in the wild, savage things that were mistaken for werewolves and centaurs but were, in fact, just mindless beasts ignorant of their abilities.

Hawk had to admit, he had never believed such stories. Spike and his sire had been fixtures in the palace for so long, he had honestly thought it not possible for any Changeling to be less than human.

They said nothing as they stood across from each other. Spike's nostrils flared in anger as he fixated on Hawk now as the reason for his rage. Hawk knew the creature was looking for a sign of repentance on his part, an acknowledgment he had somehow slighted his guardian by having feelings for the human. He searched the prince's eyes for that emotion, for even a tiny glimmer of apology. The Changeling wanted Hawk to share the same feelings for him as the creature harbored for its master.

Hawk's eyes stayed hard and cold.

"You Charmed me," Hawk said, an accusation not a question.

"I was trying to protect you," Spike pleaded.

"Protect yourself," Hawk said as he readjusted his grip on the sword.

They both instinctively knew what came next.

Without another word spoken they lunged at each other, sword and claw extended. Hawk worried about rushing into battle clad only in pants, but he knew the creature wasn't going to allow him to change into proper attire. He also knew that Spike could toughen his skin to the point of sun-cured leather, meaning anything, save actual piercing, would be useful against him. Under his breath, he recited the words for a spell of swiftness as they engaged.

Though he had little aptitude for The Arts themselves, Hawk had found an affinity for what his people referred to as Blade Dancing.

Blade Dancing was a form of combat magic that temporarily enhanced the attributes of a warrior, giving him martial abilities such as speed and strength, exceeding those of even seasoned warriors. As he repeated the short form of a series of mantras that increased concentration and focus, Hawk felt his body begin to loosen. His agility multiplied. Knowing that brute force was not going to win the battle, he used his opening attack as a feint, drawing Spike in as he nimbly flipped over the creature's back to land behind him. Caught flatfooted, the Changeling attempted to halt its charge and turn back toward his prey.

Hawk began incorporating a spell of strength into his recitation before snatching a cheap picture frame off the wall and hurling it at Spike's head. The Changeling had just managed to turn its face toward Hawk when the corner of the frame caught him on the bridge of its flat nose. Spike's head snapped back as he staggered away, his claws morphed into hands as he covered its bloody nose in what sounded like audible agony. Without a moment's hesitation or thought of mercy, Hawk reduced his body's density by almost half and launched himself upward, Truheart's hilt clutched in both hands for a killing blow.

Kane, seeing the intent, stepped out. "Hawk, no!"

Startled, the prince canceled the spell and felt his jump shorten by almost a foot as his mass returned. He landed on the floor and skidded to a halt in front of the creature's defenseless body. Kane's eyes were red-rimmed with tears, no doubt from terror. He held his hands out over Spike.

"Don't!" he pleaded. "He's down! You don't have to kill him!"

Hawk, never taking his gaze off Spike, snapped, "He's a servant, a servant who dared attack his master. Death is the least he deserves."

"He's a living being!" Kane countered, trying not to think about the fact that he sounded like every other PETA loving hippie freak in the town complaining that eating meat was murder. He knew Spike had just tried to kill him, but he also knew he was a living being, flat on his back, defenseless.

"He's just a creature," Hawk replied in an icy tone of voice, each word a shard of ice, his will icy strong.

When Kane said nothing in reply, Hawk glanced up and was shocked to see the look of abject disgust on Kane's face. It was so raw, so unexpected, Hawk felt the tip of his blade waver for a moment. "What?"

Slowly Kane took a step back from him, his expression darkening to revulsion.

"What is wrong?" Hawk asked, his voice strained, taut with emotion and the remains of battle rage. "He's a beast! A servant! I am its master! He attacked you, betrayed me! It is my right to take his life!" With each declaration the human took another step away from him. When Kane reached the stairs, he turned and fled up them, silently.

"You're losing your pet."

Hawk looked down just in time to see Spike jump up and slam his shoulder into the unprepared prince. Hawk forced himself not to cry out in shock as he went flying away from the creature, crashing into the large box that had made pictures for them earlier. He scrambled to his feet again, sure that he was about to be struck by a follow-up attack....

The room was empty, the front door open wide.

"Where did he go?" he asked Ruber, which was still floating in midair.

"Spike fled outside while you were incapacitated. It appeared wounded."

Hawk knew how Spike must feel. As he clambered to his feet, he felt several pangs lance through him and realized he was in no condition to give chase. He cursed himself for his moment of weakness as he sank down onto Kane's couch. He should have killed the thing when he had a chance. Now, a furious Changeling roamed loose on the streets of Athens, and he had no idea what it would do next.

But he knew it wasn't going to be good.

THE night air clung cool to his hide as Spike ran as quickly as he could away from the house. He could feel the trickle of blood flowing from his nose start to diminish as he began to heal.

The physical pain didn't affect him; what hurt was the pain in his chest where his heart should have been. Hawk's rejection of him for that ridiculous human was so great an insult Spike couldn't formulate words to express it.

Spike had been so sure that the prince shared some measure of the feeling he had for him, but he'd been wrong. Disastrously wrong. Worse was that his sire had warned him against harboring feelings for the royal family. He had told Spike that, in the end, he would earn nothing but heartache for his effort, and here heartache was, exactly as foretold.

In a blind rage, oblivious to everything but his fury, Spike ran to the outskirts of the town. He vowed vengeance, swore to exact retribution, vowing that the prince would one day beg for forgiveness. Even if Spike had to beat him senseless before he did so.

I SAT in my room and waited.

Remember the moment I said that I had reached my limit of things I couldn't handle and that from then on I'd be numb to anything new? Next time I say that, smack the shit out of me, okay? Hawk had meant to kill Spike, as clear and simple as buttering toast, he had been going to kill Spike with his sword. I wasn't Spike's greatest fan. I mean the—whatever it was—had just tried to kill me, but he was a living creature! I had been so sure that Hawk was a good guy—I mean what happened to arresting someone? Throwing them in prison? Who just kills someone who is defenseless on the ground?

Well, Spike had tried to do just that to me, but isn't that the point?

If Spike is a monster for trying to turn me into a happy meal, then what does it make Hawk for trying to slice and dice an enemy who was lying on his back defenseless? I wasn't mad, I was just sad because I really thought Hawk was better than that.

No—that wasn't all of it. I thought *I* was better than that and that had been what really stung.

Through the whole fight, all I'd hoped was that Hawk would cut that thing's head off. I was so scared, so outright furious, I wished for blood. Then, when I saw the same fear in Spike's eyes that I know had been in mine, the thought had hit me. That one second, that look of complete confusion on Hawk's face, though? That had been the worst. He literally had no idea why I would stop him, why I would bring up mercy. Is his whole world so different that those concepts are foreign to him? Then I stopped thinking about anything more than Hawk.

Silence filled the house, and I decided I couldn't keep hiding up here hoping everything that had happened would go away. I sneaked down the hall as quietly as I could and peeked downstairs, just knowing that Spike was going to leap out at me from the shadows. The room was empty, trashed, but empty. The front door gaped open, and I could hear the wind beginning to pick up outside. I went down a few more steps and I heard Hawk say, "He's gone, it's safe."

I saw him lying on the couch and gasped in shock.

He was cut up, badly. I ran toward him, and the damage looked worse with every step. Where he lay against it, the couch was stained with blood, meaning his back must be sliced up too. I settled on my knees next to him, wishing I could ignore how beautiful he looked, even wounded. "You're hurt," I said, afraid to touch him.

"I noticed," he said with a chuckle and then winced from the pain.

"How can I help?" I said, completely ignorant as to how to treat injuries like his.

He looked over at me, and I felt the weight of those perfect eyes again. "I thought you were mad at me."

I waved off the statement. "I am, but that doesn't mean I want you to die!"

He half smiled. "So you do care?"

I blew out a sigh in exasperation. "Is this really the time?"

He shrugged and winced again. "Might be all the time I have."

For a second I felt a stab of panic and then thought better of it. He was taking this much too well. I looked over my shoulder at Ruber. "Is he going to die?"

The ruby flicked slightly. "Eventually. But not from those wounds. The spell of healing he has cast on himself is more than capable of staving off death for another day." Ruber uttered the last words so cynically that Hawk winced.

I looked back at Hawk, pissed. "You were lying?"

"Exaggerating?" he offered.

"Why would you do that?" I said, punching him in the stomach. I was shocked to find it hard as a rock.

He flinched anyway and grabbed my hand. "I wasn't lying about the pain," he said softly.

"Why would you lie like that?"

He looked like a scolded puppy. "Two reasons. One, because you were mad at me."

"I still am," I corrected him.

He nodded and continued. "And two, you're beautiful when you're angry." He ran his hand down my cheek, and I felt my heart begin to pound in my chest like it was an alien embryo struggling to break free.

"You like me?" I asked after seconds of stunned silence.

He rolled his eyes and pulled me in toward him slowly. I felt that I could pull away and he'd let me go, that this wasn't something insistent but a question.

I leaned in toward him, the smell, the touch of his skin, everything overwhelming. I felt my head begin to spin as he leaned up. "I am Hawk'keen Maragold Tertania, prince and heir to the Arcadia throne," he said, this time a bit mockingly. "I do not like." His lips drew close to mine.

"What do you do then?" I asked, holding my breath.

His lips pressed to mine, and he showed me.

I had to admit, it felt a lot more than just *like*.

INTERLUDE

THUNDER rumbled in the distance as Spike huddled over the puddle of his own blood he'd collected. It had been easy enough to do; he merely let the wound Hawk had inflicted flow free. He buried the anger and hurt of the betrayal as he concentrated on the summoning spell. He began to incant in the guttural language that made up his people's magics, opening a connection to Faerth. When he felt the bond snap into place, he uttered his sire's true name.

The blood boiled rapidly as an image coalesced.

"Father! Hear my cries!" he said, peering deep into the pool.

His reflection shimmered slightly before it spoke back to him in the voice of his father. Without pause or preamble it asked, "It happened. Didn't it? Just as I predicted."

Spike's head bowed in shame, but the reflection did not move. He stared at him with piercing eyes as it chastised him. "I warned you that sharing feelings for those beings would gain you nothing! They hate everything that is not like them."

"I thought Hawk was different," Spike pleaded, knowing the moment he spoke the words how stupid he sounded.

"*None of them are!*" his father snapped. "The Fairies care for no one save themselves, why do you think it was so easy to manipulate the Dark to turn on them? Trust me, they have no friends."

Spike looked back into the blood, his eyes furious now. "I was wrong, Father. I should have joined you when you asked. Please, how can I help?"

The smile in the reflection was chilling as the parent reveled in its son's declaration. "You have two tasks ahead of you. One, you must find the key of Ascension; he carries it somewhere and it is the key of everything. Second, you must kill the prince. He is the rightful heir to the throne, and when we overthrow his parents, Arcadia will turn to him as leader. That's why the lord and lady sent him away, to keep him safe."

Spike nodded fervently.

"The people of Arcadia will never serve under the Dark, which is why they will need a new leader to turn to once the Lord and Lady of the realm are dead," the reflection explained. "And who better than I to lead them?"

"But you don't need him dead, you just need the key," Spike argued.

There was a long pause as his father's gaze bore into him from a world away. "Kill the prince, bring me the key. Those are my orders."

Spike nodded, breaking eye contact. "Of course, my sire."

"Once I have the key I can ascend and rule the realms once and for all."

"What of the Dark?" Spike asked, breaking his father's contemplation.

His reflection shrugged. "Who cares for the under dwellers? I simply need their numbers for now. When I am in power I will turn the full force of Arcadia against them and decimate their entire species."

"And you know the people will follow you, Father?"

"Of course they will. What choice would they have? Besides, it's not as if I do not share royal blood. Who better to rule than the royal family's regent?" The words were harsh and bitter. The topic obviously held great pain for the elder Changeling.

"I am at your command, Father," Spike said, prostrating himself to the blood.

"And soon, all of Faerth will be as well," the reflection boasted.

"Think on it, my son, you will be known as Prince Spike, heir to the throne. And I, well, I've been thinking about my title. How does Lord Puck, ruler of the nine realms sound to you?"

The reflection began to laugh as the first drops of rain began to fall.

The storm had finally arrived.

CHAPTER
TEN

MY EYES flew open when thunder crashed outside.

Startled, caught somewhere between dreaming and waking, I stared into the dark of the room. The only illumination was provided by lightning, and the irregular flashes highlighted things in strange ways, making the room I had grown up in an alien place. Confused, I tensed and started to sit up.

He shifted slightly. I felt his arm pull me closer, and everything came back to me.

We were lying on my bed in each other's arms, and I had never felt so safe in my life. I nestled back into him and could feel his breathing slow as he fell back into the deep sleep I had stirred him from. I watched the rain hit my window as I traced a circle on the taut skin over the hard muscles that made up his forearm. He was warmer than anyone I had ever felt, so much so that even above the covers I was as hot if not hotter than bundled up in a blanket. The fingers that pressed me near widened as if he was checking me even in his sleep, and I relaxed, completely safe.

We had stayed in the living room, resting on the couch, not saying a word, for several minutes after he kissed me. I sat next to him, his arm around me, his gaze never breaking with mine. I began to shiver and not from the bitter cold that rushed in through the open door. After the hectic noise of battle—I'd been in a battle!—silence flowed smoothly into the room, slowing everything: our breathing, the memories of shouting and furniture crashing. Leaving room for thought: the realization I had almost died finally began to sink in, and my shivering intensified. He shifted me even nearer to him so he could encircle me with both arms. His whisper came when I needed it the most. "Shhh. You're safe. I have you. I have you now."

I had never felt so happy to be had before.

"Y-you must think I'm a wimp. Shaking like a girl after everything's done." I gulped, pressing my face against his chest. I could hear and feel the deep, steady sound of his heart beating, and it reassured me that he was a real, flesh and blood person and not some fantasy guy I had dreamed up as a result of terminal loneliness.

"I heard the word 'wimp' which I am unsure of, but if you are afraid I think less of you for shaking after combat, you're wrong." He placed his hand over mine, and I could feel the slight tremor move through both of our limbs. "It is the adrenaline wearing off, nothing more." His lips brushed the top of my head as he whispered, "You're the bravest thing I have ever seen."

"Me?" I said, laughing in wobbly fashion at the absurdity.

I could feel him nodding. "It was wasted in a burst of absolute idiocy, but standing up for Spike, very brave."

I pulled away and looked back at him. "He is a living creature and was defenseless," I argued.

He was already shaking his head. "You're wrong, but I don't wish to fight anymore." He reached out and cupped my face. "Please." And I saw the fear and weariness in his eyes as well.

I was shocked by the notion that he could be scared also. He had seemed to be so in control, yet there fear was, reflected in his eyes. "What are we going to do?" I asked.

He shook his head and muttered miserably, "I don't know." I didn't either, so I just leaned in and kissed him. His lips were incredibly soft as they parted for me, and I felt him kiss me back. I had always thought my first kiss with a boy would be sloppy and over the top because I would want it so bad. But instead of a slobbering mess, our mouths expressed a passion that words couldn't convey. I could feel his tongue move around the surface of my lips but nothing more. This wasn't about lust or sex, this was about reassurance.

We needed to know we had each other.

"My bag!" he called out, breaking off the kiss. "I left my bag behind! If Spike gets to it...." He began to get up, but I pushed him back down. "You're half-naked, it's raining, and we have no idea where he is," I said firmly. "Ruber, can you get the bag and get back safely?" I asked.

The ruby pulsed once as it answered. "I can if that is what you wish." The voice still had that vaguely British accent that made everything sound slightly sarcastic.

"I don't want you fighting or getting hurt. Just grab his stuff, and get back here on the double."

"He can't be hurt!" Hawk argued. "He's an object."

I turned back to him and shot him a look that shouted, "Shut up!"

"It is more than possible for the Changeling to harm me, *object* or not," Ruber said, this time his voice obviously upset. His glow brightened, reacting to his outrage. "Not that you care."

"Well, I do care," I said, getting up closer to the ruby. "But if Spike gets what's in the bag, it has an even better chance of harming all of us."

The gem's light subdued a bit, I hoped that meant he was calming down. "Your logic is undeniable," it answered, bobbing in what I took as a half bow. "I will endeavor to retrieve anything of value from the domicile."

The ruby just hovered there for a moment, which made it look like it was considering my request. "I will do my best," it said, as it began to spin. I took a half step back as it vanished in a flash of light.

"What the hell is wrong with you?" I said angrily, turning to

Hawk. "He brought you here! Without him I'm dead, you wanna try to be nicer to him?"

"It," Hawk said, oblivious to my anger.

I blinked in confusion. "What?"

"It, not he."

That just pissed me off more. "It, he, or whatever, I owe Ruber my life! So cut *it* some slack, or else!" I threatened.

His smile was smug and arrogant and freaking hot. "Or what?" He raised one perfectly formed eyebrow in question.

I searched my mind for a suitable reply but found nothing. "Just be nicer, dammit!" I exclaimed as I turned to stomp off.

He grabbed my hand and stopped me. "Okay, truce!" he said, pulling me back, laughing. He kept on tugging until I sat down in his lap. My legs swung up on the couch cushions, and his face hovered over mine. "I promise to be nicer to the thing? Better?"

"He has a name," I insisted, knowing if he kissed me I was lost.

Hawk rolled his eyes as he sighed. "Fine. I promise to treat Ruber nicer. Better?"

"It's a start."

This time when he kissed me I pulled him down into it.

There was a burst of light, and thunder and rain began blowing in through the door.

"Oh crap!" I said, jumping off the couch to close it. "Not only is the place trashed, but now we're going to have water damage!" I surveyed the room and felt my stomach clench in realization of how much trouble I was going to be in. The coffee table lay in splinters, the television was smashed into the corner, and there were claws marks through the carpet that revealed deep crevices into the floor.

"Oh God!" I was dead. Suddenly, the *Home Alone* jokes didn't seem as harsh. I felt myself start to cry.

He walked up behind me, his arms wrapping around my waist. When he spoke, his voice was as solid as granite, his conviction there for me to lean against. "Everything can be fixed. You're safe, that's what matters."

"Not to my dad."

I felt his fingers intertwine with mine, and he stepped back a pace, turned, and led me toward the stairs. "Come," he said softly. "This day needs to end."

I just didn't have the energy to argue with him, and I let him lead me upstairs to my room. He started to lead us to my bed, and I stopped.

"Um, you aren't laying on my bed in those," I said, pointing at his jeans.

"Very well," he said, starting to unbutton them.

"*No!*" I cried out, averting my eyes. "I mean those pants are trashed, you need to put something else on."

"But I don't have anything else." His fingers stilled at the buttons.

After what seemed to be an hour of arguing but was really maybe five minutes, I had persuaded him to switch his jeans out for a pair of shorts so they could be washed. When he had walked out of the bathroom wearing a pair of sweats I cut down into shorts I felt my jaw do a dive toward the floor in shock. In the middle of the fight I had subconsciously noticed his body, but the whole Changeling-trying-to-kill-me-thing had kind of put the memory of what I'd seen on the back burner. Standing in my bathroom doorway, handing me his jeans, I could see every line I had missed before. Every visible muscle on his body was exposed in perfect detail. Even simple movements resulted in a mesmerizing play of light and shadow. He looked as if he was flexing his entire body at once. It took me a second to get through my head the understanding that what I was seeing was him essentially at rest. Then I prayed I never saw him strike a pose. I had no desire to recover from a stroke, no matter how hot the cause.

"What?" he asked, when all I did was stare for a few seconds in awe. "I look ridiculous, don't I?" He turned back to the bathroom. "I knew this was a mistake; one doesn't wear rags!"

"No! Wait!" I choked, grabbing his shoulder with my hand. It felt like grabbing a furnace when I turned him around. My fingers tightened on solid muscle, every part of him hard, perfect. I hesitantly trailed my hand down his chest, moving in the cleft between his pecs and pausing at the pendant he wore. It was an acorn that looked as if it were made of solid gold, which after what he had said about his world probably was. "You look incredible," I murmured as my fingertips traced the ridges that made up his abs. I had never known that a human body could feel like his. "You're perfect," I added absently, not even talking to him anymore.

His hand covered mine, and I looked back at his face. I could see the warmth in his expression, could feel it wrapping around my fingers, traveling from his hand to my hand and then through the rest of me. He smiled reflectively and nodded, devastating as he replied, "Of course I am. I'm the heir of the Arcadian throne."

I closed my mouth when I realized I had been waiting for him to return the compliment. "Well at least you know you're perfect." I tried to push away from him, but he held me fast.

"Of course I am perfect," he said, his voice low with emotion as his face pressed to mine. "It is the blessing of my people, nothing more."

"I'm not perfect," I said, wondering what in the world I was doing with a guy who looked like this.

"Perhaps you are to me." His smile and his words were genuine, and I felt my heart skip a beat. Then he kissed me, and my heart thudded double time through a lot more than one beat.

"Are you cold?" he asked. I realized I'd fallen half-asleep watching the rain.

I shook my head as my eyes closed again. "No."

He kissed my temple, and I felt the warm rush of affection move over me as I dozed off.

HE WOKE up staring at the window, his vision blurry for a moment as he struggled to orient himself without waking Kane in turn.

The storm had built up momentum and ferocity. Sheets of rain accompanied by howls of wind slammed against the glass, but they were not what had roused him. The sky was dark outside the window, and except for spatters of illumination provided by brief flashes of lightning, not even the tree next to the house was visible. The light woke Kane momentarily but Hawk could tell the boy was drifting off, his arms were folded across his chest as if cradling something.

"Are you cold?" Hawk whispered, gauging how awake Kane was.

"No," the boy answered drowsily. After a few seconds, Kane's breathing evened out, and he obviously fell back to sleep. Hawk leaned forward and kissed his temple. Smiling against Kane's hair when he turned his head into the caress.

Hawk waited for the boy to sink deeper into slumber before disengaging himself from their embrace. He slowly eased off the bed, listening to the human's breathing before every move.

He paused at the side of the bed, looking down at him and wondered what he was doing, startled at the depth of his feelings for someone he'd only met a few days before.

Clinically, he would say that he was desperate and alone in a strange world and that the human's affection provided him with a crutch. He could rationalize that the romantic feelings he was experiencing were, in truth, a desire for some kind of connection in this trash heap of a world and that those feelings were exaggerated by the stress of his situation. If he were a Healer, he might say that there was nothing about Kane that would continue to attract him once things calmed and he adjusted to the world around him. And if he were a Healer, he'd point out the logic of his arguments.

He might say all of that if he didn't know in his heart how much he already cared. Didn't know that the logical approach was wrong on every level he could imagine.

Hawk took the blanket that was folded at the foot of the bed and draped it over Kane, careful not to wake him. Without a sound, he walked across the room to the window. The storm raged against the glass, shaking it as the wind shifted.

He should leave. Every second he was with Kane, he put the human in danger. Spike's jealousy would know no bounds, and it was just a matter of time before the creature attacked again.

And if Hawk left—he clenched his fists against the pain that notion caused—the boy was still in danger.

There was no guarantee the Changeling would follow him if he fled the town. Spike had already attacked Kane once, and Hawk knew there were no guarantees that it wouldn't attempt the same thing again. If he was honest, he didn't know whether the possibility of having Hawk to itself on the road was enough of a lure. Spike might follow him, after he'd done away with Kane. He had to make a choice and make it quickly. If he was to leave, he needed to be gone before Kane woke up. He would never leave once he looked into Kane's eyes; that much was clear. Struggling with his choice, he rested his forehead against the window and focused outside. Something out of place caught and held his attention. Squinting, he looked down at the rain-soaked outer windowsill.

In the wood, there were fresh claws marks, three claws to a foot. Suddenly, Hawk knew what had alerted him. Spike had been watching them slumber. Mere steps from an easily opened or broken window, Spike had been staring at them. At Kane. Hawk's left fist slammed down on his leg at just the notion that Kane might be harmed. In that instant, Spike made Hawk's mind up for him.

IN HIS dire wolf form, Spike howled miserably as he loped down the street. Spike had gone back to give Hawk one more chance to change his mind before things went too far. When he had spied the two of them asleep on the bed together, Spike had known that the situation had already strayed out of its control. He burst through the wooden door of the abandoned house they had been staying in as if it was paper. The minor act of destruction satisfied a tithe of his anger. Bent on taking Hawk's pack and leaving with it, perhaps so that Hawk would follow and retrieve it, Spike glanced up and skidded to a halt in surprise.

The ruby floated at head level as various objects around the room floated toward it and into the pack. "Hello, Spike," it said in an overly cheerful tone.

The Changeling hissed in anger as it leapt at the artifact.

It collided with a pale red shield that surrounded the ruby; in a matter of seconds, Spike landed on the floor in a stunned heap. "Make no mistake. The fact that I cannot initiate offensive actions against you does not mean that I cannot defend myself."

Spike shook his stupor off, and he morphed a human mouth onto the wolf's head. "Why are you here, gemling?"

"I am collecting the prince's belongings. The question *is*, what are you doing here?" Spike loathed the condescending tone in the gem's voice; he always had. "Your service to him is done, there are no ties keeping you on this world." The ruby floated closer to him. "So why are you still here?"

"The prince—" Spike began and was immediately cut off by Ruber.

"You attacked the prince and tried to slay his... well, consort, I suppose. The next time he sees you he will run you through with his sword."

Spike snarled as he paced around the gem's shield. "And what about you? How much do you think you are valued, given away as a gift. Twice."

The room grew silent as the two magical creatures stared at each other. Finally, Ruber pulled the satchel nearer to him. "Go home, Spike. If you know what's good for you, leave this place and never look back." The glow around him began to intensify as he opened the portal back to Kane's home. "There is no way you can get to the boy with Hawk guarding him. We both know you cannot best him in combat." There was a rush of air as the gem and pack vanished from the room, leaving Spike to meditate on the ruby's words.

WHEN Ruber appeared back inside Kane's house, he was shocked to find Hawk trying to sweep up the wreckage that had once been the human's living room. "Your gear, majesty," the ruby announced, depositing his bundle on the couch.

"My thanks," the prince growled as he fumbled with the broom. "Is there an enchantment for this? So far nothing is cleaner!"

"May I ask what you are doing?"

Hawk looked over at the ruby in confusion. "What does it look like I am doing?" he snarled.

"Making a moderate fool of yourself with a broom," the gem answered with more than a little sarcasm.

Hawk's glare was withering. "Do I have to remind you I am still heir to—"

"The Arcadian throne, yes, I am all too aware. Must I remind you I am not your property and that we are not in Arcadia?"

Hawk tossed the broom down. "I know exactly where I am, and I don't care if you are my property or not. I am a prince, and I won't be addressed—"

"So am I," the ruby interjected, stopping Hawk in midsentence.

"What?"

"I am considered a prince in my lands, yet you have addressed me in far worse terms."

Hawk tried to find an answer, stumbling over his words. "It's different, I mean, you are a gem, and I am—it doesn't matter! We are not in your lands, so what does it matter?" he blurted out.

"My point exactly," Ruber said, floating directly in front of the prince's face.

Hawk considered swinging at the insolent artifact, but he knew it was right. Instead, he knelt down and retrieved the broom.

"Again, I must ask, what are you doing?" Ruber asked.

"I am attempting to tidy up some of the destruction I have brought to his house." Hawk went back to trying to get the broom to clean up the room by moving it over the debris. "It is my fault it came to this, and I feel the need to make restitution."

"Because you are honor bound," Ruber stated, not asked.

"Because Kane should not have to pick up my mess after me," he clarified.

Neither spoke for several minutes as the prince tried to find the magic of the device, and the gem looked on in amazement. "If I lived another hundred thousand years I would have never thought to see such a sight."

"What?" the prince snapped, not looking up from his task.

"An Arcadian noble attempting to wield a broom."

Hawk turned to take issue with the floating gem. Instead, the magical device slipped between him and the broom. A brief click and the broom hummed with power. The broom hovered upright next to Ruber, awaiting orders. "You are aware Spike is not going to give up?" the ruby asked as it began to manipulate the broom.

Hawk nodded. "It desires the human's death."

"The house can be warded against intrusion, but it is a stopgap at best. The boy's father will be home soon, and you two must leave at some point."

Hawk collapsed into the large chair sighing wearily. "I know."

"You must take the fight to the Changeling," Ruber said, gathering a pile of wreckage. "It is the only logical choice."

"You think I don't know that?" he growled back. "If Kane had allowed me to slay Spike in the first place, this would be a moot point."

The ruby continued to talk as it manipulated the broom around the wreckage. "Yes, but of course, slaying a defenseless foe that is flat on its back is not exactly what I would call honorable combat."

"The creature attacked an unarmed human! How honorable do you call that?" Hawk retorted.

"Ah," the gem said, casting a reconstruction spell on the pile beneath it. "But Spike is just a creature, and you are the heir to the Arcadian throne." The pieces began to reconstitute themselves into their original forms under the careful ministrations of the ruby. "If there is a difference besides simply a title, what is it?"

"What do you mean?" he asked, leaning forward in the chair.

"I mean, if he is a monster for attacking a defenseless foe, what does that make you for trying to do the same?"

Hawk sat in silence as he realized he had no idea how to answer.

CHAPTER ELEVEN

I WOKE up alone.

The rain seemed to have eased off when I stared at the window and tried to figure out if the past few days had been a dream or not. Was I Dorothy? Imagining a world I wasn't in control of only to find out I was a klutz and had fallen into a pig pen, cracked my head open, and imagined the whole thing?

The thought of Hawk not being real was terrifying.

I jumped out of bed and raced out of my room. When I got to the top of the stairs I could see the living room. The unreality of the whole situation spiraled sharply upward. Everything was just as it was supposed to be. No broken table, no ripped carpet, nothing. The TV was fine; in fact, it was on, playing an old cartoon. I took a few more halting steps, wondering how Hawk could have seemed so real, lost because I'd imagined the entire thing—

His laugh echoed across the room, and I felt the clenching of my stomach relax so quickly my head spun.

I reached the foot of the stairs and saw him sitting on the couch laughing like a loon at the figures on the screen. He looked over at me and pointed at the television. "Have you seen this? These creatures are insane!" Amid his laughter, he smiled at me and waved me nearer to him.

I took a few hesitant steps into the living room, looking for evidence of last night's battle. There was nothing; if anything it looked cleaner than it had been. "What happened?" I asked in wonderment.

"I cleaned up," Hawk said proudly.

"*I* cleaned up," Ruber corrected him.

"We cleaned up," Hawk amended.

"I don't understand…," I said, looking around in a circle.

"Magic."

I looked over at Hawk.

"We used—"

"*I* used," Ruber interrupted him.

"*We* used magic."

I sighed and sat down in my dad's chair. "Okay, I think we need to talk."

"But the creatures are dancing!" he said, pointing to the TV.

"They're cartoons," I explained.

"I have tried to explain animation to him, but he is uninterested," Ruber commented dryly.

I reached over and grabbed the remote and turned it off. "We need to talk."

He tried to hide the disappointment as he turned to me. "You have questions."

I nodded. "I just want to know what is going on before I fall any deeper down this rabbit hole."

He cocked his head in confusion.

"*Alice in Wonderland?*" Blank look. "Little girl falls down a rabbit hole and ends up in a weird place with playing cards and a talking rabbit?" Now an incredulous look. "Red Queen? Off with your head?"

He nodded instantly at that. "It sounds like Aponiviso, ruled by the Family Crimson." I just stared, my mind in disarray. "Are we speaking of the same place?"

I got up and walked over to the small bookcase my father kept in the corner. I picked through the titles and found his collected works of Lewis Carroll. I handed it over to Hawk. "No. I was referring to a character in a book."

He took it but didn't open it. "I have no way of reading this without the bauble."

I removed the back of the earring and handed both over to him. The second he attached it to his ear I saw his face change, no doubt the words on the cover suddenly making sense. He flipped through the book, taking pause at each illustration and studying it.

"You're from there?" I asked, knowing the question was insane.

He shook his head gravely as he continued to skim the book. "No, but it reminds me of Aponiviso. It is a broken world; the laws no longer work, so things like gravity and dimensions change from moment to moment. Some seem flat as cards while others are enormous for no reason at all!" He turned the book around and pointed to a drawing of the White Rabbit. "This looks like Farnsworth, royal page and messenger for the Family Crimson. The device in his hand has the ability to manipulate time and space."

"It's a timepiece," I said, knowing the picture well. I had grown up with these books, my father having a healthy interest in fairy tales and everything else most people deemed to be completely useless.

He shook his head. "It is a piece of time."

We both stared at the book for a minute without speaking. It was obvious neither one of us knew what was going on. I got up and pulled down a copy of *The Lion, The Witch and The Wardrobe*. I flipped through it, pausing at an illustration of the Ice Queen. I handed it to him.

His eyes went wide in shock. "This looks like Queen Pudani of Niflgard!" He looked over to Ruber and asked, "What sorcery is this?"

For the first time, the ruby did not sound so sure of its answer. "I am not sure," it began hesitantly. "That is an accurate rendering of Pudani, but that is impossible. When was this book published?"

"1950s, I think." Though Ruber had no face, I imagined its silence was akin to Hawk's confusion. "About sixty years ago," I tried.

"Yet The Abandonment was...," Hawk began, doing some kind of calculation in his head.

"Nearly fifteen hundred years ago," Ruber answered for him. "It is difficult to be sure with the time differential between the realms." He seemed almost apologetic that he had to be so vague.

"Then what is this?" Hawk asked, holding up the book.

"I am no closer to answering that question than I was the first time you asked," the floating gem answered with more than a little resentment. I guess he didn't like not knowing something.

"Okay, I am really no closer to understanding what the hell is going on," I said, interrupting their conversation.

Hawk put the book down as Ruber floated over to the bookcase. "Well, I am Hawk'keen Maragold Tertania, son to Titania and Oberon, rulers of Arcadia and Lords of Faerth."

He waited for me to say something, but honestly, most of the words he just said sounded like a strange mix of French and Latin. When he saw my incomprehension his hands began to reach for the earring, but Ruber stopped him. "I am capable of the same enchantment as the bauble possesses, I believe you both will need your native comprehension to make sense of this."

Ruber floated back toward me, and as he did, he began to shrink smaller and smaller until he was the same size as the emerald in Hawk's ear. I felt it wiggle into the hole in my lobe and hold itself there. I was about to check if it was in place when I felt the tingle of magic move through me, much more powerful than the magic the earring made.

"Okay, say that again," I said to Hawk.

"I am Hawk'keen Maragold Tertania, son to Titania and Oberon, rulers of Arcadia and Lords of Faerth." The accent was gone now, and the names were instantly recognizable. "*The* Titania and Oberon?" I asked in awe.

"You know of my parents?" he asked, leaning forward quickly.

"They are in the play!" I said, looking for my backpack before realizing it had been burned in the theater. "We're doing that play for the spring production," I explained quickly. "The costumes that attacked us were from *A Midsummer Night's Dream*."

I could tell the name meant nothing to Hawk, but I could see him recalling something. "The uniforms were familiar somehow, but I thought them shoddy replicas or perhaps from an army without sufficient funds for complete outfitting. To say they come from a play makes their appearance understandable but no less confusing."

"Wait!" I said, wracking my brain for what little I knew of the play. "The queen, Titania, there was argument about a child—" And my face paled. "A shape shifter."

It was obviously the wrong thing to say, as Hawk's eyes flashed in anger and I could see his face redden. "How. Do. You. Know. Of. That?" he demanded.

I held up my hands to calm him down. "It's a story. Well, it is here. You're from the realm of fairies?" I asked in disbelief.

He was still glaring at me, but somehow I knew he was angrier at the shame of what I had just said than at me specifically. It was like being told that your family's dirty laundry was aired for school children to read and laugh at. Ruber's voice came from between us even though he was still in my ear. "Your majesty," he began carefully, "I know you are upset, but only through communication are we going to get any closer to understanding—"

"I am from Faerth," Hawk said, cutting him off. "Our people are called fairies." His voice was harsh, but I could tell he was trying to calm himself. He shot me a nervous smile, distracted by what he was reading, but not so far away that he didn't want to reassure me.

"But I don't understand. How are these books in my world real places in your world?" I asked, still not getting it.

"We are the heart of the nine worlds," Hawk began. "They are all bound to us since we are the center of the universe; they are not from our world, but they are known to us."

I shook my head. "Even with Ruber helping, that made no sense."

He looked around and grabbed a pad of paper and a pencil from the end table. He put it down and began to draw silently. I watched, knowing interrupting him would only take up time. He spun the pad around and showed me the crude drawing he'd made. It looked like a cross with his world in the center of it.

"Faerth is the center world. All eight other worlds are tethered to us, crossing over with our world yet worlds unto themselves," he tried to explain.

Ruber added, "There are places on Faerth that intersect the other worlds, allowing free travel from one realm to another as long as a traveler passes through Faerth first."

I pointed at the gap that was just underneath the center world of the circle. "Why does there seem to be one missing?" I asked.

"There is," Hawk said, putting the pencil in the middle of the space. "That is where your world was."

I tried to absorb that my world had been somewhere I'd never heard of. "Wait, was?"

Ruber's voice answered, "The connection with your world was severed over a millennium ago."

"We used to be able to travel to fairyland?"

"Faerth," Hawk corrected me. "The facilitation place used to be called...." He snapped his fingers trying to remember. "...something with an A...."

"Avalon," Ruber provided.

"Yes!" Hawk said excitedly. "There was a place called Avalon where one would cross over with our world. But it was deemed your people were incapable of coexisting with the other nine worlds without incessant war, hence The Abandonment."

I stared down at the paper. I couldn't take my eyes off of the blank space on the circle. "So then what are these worlds?" I asked, dazed.

He began at the top of the cross and began to name them. "This is Tokpewa, Aponiviso, this is of course Faerth, and here, Niflgard, with Helgard on its shoulder."

He looked like he was going to go on, but I stopped him. "Okay, this is weird!" I said, standing quickly. "So you come from a place where fairy tales are true and magic is normal and where my world used to exist, but doesn't now." I looked at Hawk. "I don't know if I can handle all this."

Hawk rose slowly, his voice was calm and soothing, like he was talking to a wild animal. "I know this is strange for you. It's strange for me. But I know it is not beyond your understanding."

"You got this wrong!" I panted loudly, forcing a word out on each exhale. Then, when his expression didn't become more threatening, bundles of words, rather than just one, escaped. "I'm not that guy, I am not the guy who can just accept that everything I know about my world isn't right!"

He crossed the three steps to me and put his hands on my shoulders, wrapping his fingers about them and anchoring me. "Yes. You are." He smiled at me, and I felt my panic begin to lessen.

"Why do you think that?" I pleaded with him.

"I don't think, I know." His voice was firm with conviction as he stared straight into my eyes, looking right through the skin and into me.

"How?"

"Because you're stronger than you can imagine, Kane. You put yourself between me and a creature that had been trying to kill you last night. There was no question in your mind that it deserved mercy. And whether it had just tried to kill you didn't matter. That it is a Changeling and I am of Faerth. These are things you have accepted without question. You have already proved it."

"Proved what?"

"That you can accept great challenges, great changes. You already have." When he saw my face, he understood I wasn't following him. "Kane, look around you! You knew that the earring was magical, you accept that Ruber is alive and talking, you've already accepted it, you just don't know it yet. You're stronger than you think. Give yourself some credit."

"I was terrified last night," I corrected him.

"Well, you didn't seem scared, which just shows how much you can overcome." He leaned in and rested his forehead against mine. "You can do this." His body trembled just once, and he added, "And you're all I have."

The pain in his voice was so real that my arms reached around him, pulling him closer, willing away the vast loneliness behind his words. I sighed as I thought about his words; if I was going to have a heart attack or something, I would have done it when the shape shifting thing thought I was kibbles and bits. Little late to wuss out now.

And besides that, he was right. I was all he had.

"So what do we do now?" I asked, dreading the answer.

"Eat?" he offered eagerly. "But not scraps."

He was too cute not to kiss.

SPIKE destroyed the interior of the house out of sheer spite.

He hated this world, he hated that he had lost Hawk, he hated that puny human, and he hated that the damn ruby had been right. He didn't know what he was still doing here if he wasn't going to kill Hawk. The Changeling paused at that thought, could he do it? Could he really snuff the life out of the prince?

He screamed in frustration again as he picked up the rotted bed he'd found upstairs and prepared to throw it across the room. There was a broken mirror still hanging on the wall, and Spike saw his reflection within its shattered surface grinning back at him. Then his reflection's lips moved when his own didn't. "Well, I see you're spending your time constructively."

Spike dropped the bed and moved near to the mirror. "Father?"

"*Of course it's me!*" Puck raged back at him. "Is the prince dead?" Before Spike could even open his mouth Puck kept talking, "Wait, let me answer for you. No, not yet, Father, I am too weak to actually finish the task because I am a failure." The reflection of his own eyes glared at him. "Say I am wrong."

Spike swallowed hard as he shrank away from his father's image.

"I knew it. I am sending a group of people to make sure this gets done. You're done there."

"Wait!" Spike called out as his reflection began to turn away from him. "I can do it. I will do it. I just need time, Father, he is prepared for me."

"More reason to send professionals," Puck countered.

"I will do it!" he bellowed.

The two of them stared at each other for a couple of silent minutes. Finally Puck said, "You have one week—human time—to finish this. Seven days and I am sending a cadre of assassins to end this one way or another." The reflection leaned closer to the glass. "And, Spike, if the prince is not dead when they arrive, I suggest running. Fast."

Spike said nothing as the reflection flickered back to just to an image of himself.

He stood there gulping, heaving lungfuls of air as he struggled not to lash out at the offending mirror in rage. Seven days, seven days to kill the prince.

"I can do this," Spike said to himself as he let his form relax.

He stood almost four feet tall with a curve to his spine that made him hunch forward. His arms were longer than a human's so his knuckles touched the floor. His legs hinged similar to a goat's but he had three sharp talons on his feet instead of hooves. He was covered with a fine pelt of light brown fur that could be mistaken for a wolf's pelt at a distance. His face was wide and his jaw jutted out past his upper lip. Two large fangs pointed upward to his luminous yellow eyes. His ears came out to the side like a doe's and had a ring of darker fur around the edge.

He rarely took his true form, preferring to be nearly any other animal instead of his deformed collection of body parts. He focused as he attempted to stand up straight. His back fought him, but he clenched his teeth and concentrated past the pain.

Slowly, he balanced in his new upright position. To take his mind from the pain of stretched and abused muscles, joints, and nerves, he concentrated on the remainder of the transformation. The fur began to fade, revealing rapidly lightening skin underneath. His claws retracted and vanished altogether and he grew another two toes. His arms shrank, and the talons on both hands began to reduce in size.

He screamed again, this time in pain, as he forced his form farther than he ever had before.

I HAD to smile as I watched him scour the breakfast menu at Mr. Watson's.

He looked so—I don't even know if there is a word to describe the way he looked. He was handsome, of course, but his eyes looked as if they belonged to a child as he excitedly read each dish to himself off the menu and then licked his lips. His exuberance at just the thought of food made my heart feel as if it was swelling in my chest.

"It's exciting to be able to read the—what did you call it?" he asked, holding up the menu.

"A menu."

"A menu, yes. Usually it's written on a slate or the serving girl just tells you," he commented, going back to the list. "What is tofu?" he asked, turning the menu over and pointing to the word.

"Um…," I said, not sure what tofu was now that I thought about it. "Best to stick to an omelet right now," I recommended, not sure how he'd take eating a protein substitute.

"Eggs, cheese, and onions?" he read to me, verifying that was what I meant.

"Close enough," I confirmed, not even wanting to go into what the eggs really were. I never noticed how hard explaining what a vegan diet consisted of before that moment.

Wanda, the part owner, came up to our table with a huge smile. "I know you're ready, Kane. What about your very cute friend?"

I blushed as I handed her my menu. My dad and I ate here so much they knew what I had for each meal by heart now. Hawk looked at her with an intense stare for way too long before saying, "Did you just make a comment about my looks?"

She nodded. "Hard to miss them, cutie. So what you have?"

He looked back at me, and in a voice that was more than audible to Wanda asked, "Is this servant addressing me with familiarities?"

I saw the look of disbelief on Wanda's face as I grabbed the menu out of his hand. "He'll have the same," I said, ignoring him.

She looked down at him as she took the menu from my hand, every motion deliberate. He opened his mouth to say something to her, and I kicked him under the table as hard as I could.

"*Ouch!*" he cried in shock. "You kicked me!"

"Thanks, Wanda." I gave her my biggest grin. She walked away slowly, never taking her eyes off of Hawk. Once she was out of earshot I looked at him. "What is wrong with you? You can't talk to people like that!"

"You are mistaken. I can and will." His voice was louder than I liked, and the few diners looked at us in confusion.

"Shut up!" I hissed, trying to slump down in the booth. "People are staring at us."

"So?" he cried, looking around. "Let them stare, as if I would care that people such as…."

"She was taking your order," I said, trying not to lose my temper. "You didn't act like this at all last night!"

"The other woman didn't address me as if we were equals," he said, and then paused. "Did she? If she did you should have told me."

"You can't treat people like that."

"And servants should not—" he began to recite.

I had no idea what was going to follow that, but I knew it wasn't going to be good. I ducked out of the booth and pulled him out as I headed toward the door. "Be right back!" I called out to Wanda, who was standing by the order window talking to her partner, the cook, Linda. Once outside, I spun on him. "Okay, look! I have no idea why you started acting like this, but you have to stop!" He looked as if I slapped him, but I didn't care. "Those are people, real people! You can't just talk down to them."

"I can," he answered simply as he began to count off on his fingers. "One, I am above them, so I can surely talk down to them. Two, I am far better looking, which means that my opinion—"

"You're better looking?" I exploded, interrupting his list. "What the hell does that have to do with anything?"

He paused a few seconds before explaining, as if I was a child. "Because the better looking a person is, the more status they have."

He could have said he was also secretly a Nazi, and I would have been less shocked.

"Are you serious?"

"He very much is," Ruber said in my ear.

"Your culture is based on how good-looking someone is?" There was literally no more outrage that could be crammed into my tone of voice. "*That* is what you base things on?"

"On perfection," he tried to explain. "Which physical beauty is a large part of, yes. I am royalty, and she is of working class—"

"She is the owner, you asshole!" I shouted over him.

"She is the owner of a tavern," he corrected me. "And one that cannot even provide actual eggs, so I am not sure how good a tavern it is."

"And she is a friend," I added, trying to calm myself down because I was sure everyone in the diner was looking out the window at our fight. Quick glance over... yep, all looking. Awesome. "You are a guest here. Not a prince, not royalty, not anything. You get that?" From the look on his face, he didn't. "Lemme ask you this, how were you going to pay for the meal? You have any money on you?"

In a very low voice, he said, "My meals are usually gifts—"

"And if you couldn't pay for what you ate, you know what they would have done? Made you wash dishes to pay it off!" You'd swear I told him that he was going to have to have sex with pigs from the look of disgust on his face. "You aren't in your world anymore, and the sooner you stop acting like you're better than everyone else...." He began to respond, but I overrode him again. "... *and* realize you are not better than everyone else, the quicker people will stop thinking you are a douche bag."

He turned pale, and his eyes looked like they were going to fall out of their sockets. "Why would you need a bag—for—" He turned toward the street. "I think I am going to be sick." I watched him puke into the gutter, holding his stomach as he heaved.

"Sometimes the most literal translations are the best," Ruber said in my ear, and I tried not to smile.

"You are going to go in there and apologize to Wanda or I swear to all that is holy—"

"I will! I will!" he said, holding a hand up for me to stop. "Just please do not mention containers that are for...." And he began throwing up again.

"Well done, Ruber," I murmured.

"Thank you," it responded, obviously loving Hawk's reaction.

CHAPTER TWELVE

JEWEL sat in Donde está Da Bean trying to drown her sorrow in a double sweet, extra foam latte, wishing she wasn't as furious as she was. Looking at the mug on the table in front of her only made her sadder because she and Kane had had a Saturday ritual forever. They'd come in, both order their favorite coffee, and then mix the two of them to make truly horrible mugs of coffee that were unique and *theirs*. She began tearing the corner of her napkin, shredding it meticulously as she turned it around and around in her hand. There were already two piles of paper piled up next to her mug; this one would be the third.

She knew she shouldn't be feeling betrayed, but what she knew and what she was feeling were two different things.

She had been friends with Kane ever since she could remember. There wasn't a memory of Athens that wasn't somehow connected to him. In all that time she had believed she knew him, but obviously, she'd been wrong. The person she knew would never have blown her off to go to the movies with a boy. Even if the boy was hotter than just about everyone on the planet combined. Halfway through her napkin, she felt her eyes tear up.

Jewel had heard of friends drifting apart when a boyfriend or girlfriend entered the picture. She didn't want to think this would happen to them. Even though Kane was better looking than she was, she had assumed the lack of other gay kids in the town would put their chances of finding someone about even, somewhere near nil. She knew there was no way she could get a guy, even a guy who was as open-minded as the ones in Athens were. Every other girl was a rail thin vegetarian that looked like a strong wind could knock them down.

Her napkin lay in a neat heap of tiny pieces near its siblings. Jewel realized that she was taking a bubble bath in emotional self-pity. And she had absolutely no intention of stopping until the last bubble had escaped down the drain. How trite: fat girl sits alone, crying her eyes out. Jewel hated the way that idea sounded. It was such a stereotype that she felt like puking.

Kane had always been her shield, her impromptu boyfriend, standing between her and the crushing weight of being a high-school outcast. The two of them liked to ridicule the town and its absurdities. Part of the reason Jewel mocked Athens was because she knew she would never find love here. All the girls were vegans, annoyingly in shape, cliquish as their PTA perfect mothers had been before them. Jewel knew logically that her weight hovered near average for her height, but logic flew out the window when she looked at the popular girls.

She had always known Kane was as desperate as she was for a boyfriend. She just hadn't been prepared for him to find one, much less one as hot as the guy she had seen him at the movies with. She was still confused on where the guy had come from. Kane had said he had just started at Quince, but as of yesterday morning, not one person, other than Kane, had said a word about him. None of it made any sense to her. She got up and retrieved another stack of napkins from the condiment bar.

All she knew was there was a hot guy, and Kane hated her.

She didn't want to know much more than that to be honest. She was miserable, and right now, that suited her perfectly. As she sat back down, her hand slipped into her pocket and pulled out her ever-present iPod. Running on memory, she let her fingers scroll through her playlists. She had created a playlist for every emotion she might experience in a typical day. She zipped past sad, angry, depressed, and stopped on heartbroken.

She had never had to use that particular playlist before, but she didn't miss the irony involved in making a heartbroken playlist, just in case.

She stared glumly into her latte and swirled the foam around with her straw as the Carpenters began to wail into her ears. Completely consumed by her self-inflicted misery, she lost herself in her music. Which was why she never saw him coming.

AFTER a series of heartfelt apologies given to Wanda, her partner, and the other people in the diner, Hawk sat back down in the booth and waited quietly for the food to arrive. He looked upset, and I felt bad for the way I snapped at him. But I didn't feel bad enough to let the topic go. I needed to understand something that struck me as idiotic, but that was, apparently, the basis of Hawk's way of life.

"So your whole society is based on perfection?" I asked after a few minutes of uncomfortable silence. He nodded solemnly but didn't add anything to his answer as he pretended to examine the street outside. "How does that work?"

He looked back to me, and I saw his eyes were now ice blue. "Why should I tell you anything? So you can judge and mock my way of life some more?"

I sighed, realizing this argument was going nowhere; when a thought crossed my mind, I did a mental double take. "Because according to our standards, your way of life sounds shallow. But you aren't shallow." And I knew I'd hit what had been bothering me since the topic had come up. "You aren't shallow; I want to understand. Please."

"Shallow?" he asked a little too loudly as Wanda glared over the diner at him. In a whisper he asked again. "Shallow? So my way of life is shallow but the human way, *your* way is deep and perfect, right?"

"I didn't say that!" I countered. "But we just don't pick who is more important based on something as stupid as looks."

"Really?" he said, the anger in his voice growing. I was about to answer when he left the booth and walked over to the counter. He flipped through a stack of magazines to read while-you-waited, grabbed one, and strode back to me. "Spike had found some of these in the house where we were," he explained as he opened a *People* magazine to a picture of Brad Pitt. "So this man must have cured a disease or is a mighty warrior to command ten million dollars a movie. A movie is one of the frozen plays such as we saw yesterday, correct?" I nodded, although I'm not sure he noticed, since he kept on talking. "I am assuming that ten million dollars is a lot of money, but I haven't quite figured out your currency system yet. Forgive me if I am incorrect. But if what I read is correct, this man makes an exorbitant sum of money for doing nothing more than being handsome. How is that different?" Before I could answer he flipped the page to a picture of Angelia Jolie. "It says this woman commands the same amount of money, so together they must be like a king and queen. Am I right? And while we are at it, please tell me what a Kardashian is."

"I wish I knew." I mumbled as I looked down at the myriad of pictures of beautiful people staring blankly back at me and tried to find an answer that didn't taste like ass in my mouth. "They make a lot of money, but we don't follow them—"

"Your entire society is built on the acquisition of material goods, and those goods are procured with money, correct?" he asked.

"Yes, but that is not what leadership is built on." I tried to explain. Hawk realized he still stood staring down at me and immediately sat opposite me.

"According to the teacher at the academy, your country is based on a system of privately owned companies that are run for profit. So doesn't that mean this Pitt fellow and his wife make the most profit? And if they aren't your leaders and in charge, does the person who does lead you make more than they do?"

"Well, no. But they aren't our leaders," I said, wondering what his conclusion was to be and not liking the possibilities.

"So your society is based on money, and you give the most

money to the prettiest people. Your leaders make less money than the pretty people who, unlike the best looking people in my world, are not trained to lead. So the rich, pretty people are 'idols' because they're rich and pretty? And useless," he said, sitting down across from me.

I opened my mouth to say something when the other people in the diner began to clap. Cries of "You tell them! Capitalism sucks, man!" echoed throughout the restaurant as they thought Hawk just another eccentric hippie.

He looked around, smiling, not knowing why he was being celebrated but enjoying it nonetheless.

"Oh brother," I said under my breath.

"He did seem to take that round," Ruber commented as Hawk nodded and waved to the people.

Our food couldn't come fast enough.

JEWEL looked up and realized someone was watching her.

There was a guy sitting at one of the corner tables, staring intently straight at her. Jewel knew beyond a shadow of a doubt that she'd never seen him before, because if she had, she would've never taken her eyes off of him. He had dark features, Indian brown skin, long black hair, and pair of smoldering dark eyes that seemed to absorb the light from around him. He had a well-worn black leather jacket on that just screamed rock and roll to her. He was part James Dean, part Marlon Brando, and part Sid Vicious in one sexy package.

He hadn't looked away when she looked back.

Realizing she was staring, she lowered her eyes and looked for a fresh napkin to shred. She peeked up and, sure enough, he was still looking at her. He flashed her a tight grin. For some reason, his smile made her imagine what a wolf would look like if it could smile. She felt a rush of excitement as she looked down again. Who was this guy? Where did he come from? Was he really looking at her? When she stole another glance, she was startled to see him standing at the edge of her table. He wasn't drinking coffee, didn't have any food in his hand, in fact, he didn't seem to be doing anything but watching her.

She slipped off her ear buds and looked at him expectantly.

"You're listening to Music?" he asked. His voice was deep and rich with the slightest hint of an accent she couldn't place.

It was obvious that English wasn't his first language by the way he emphasized the word music. She smiled and nodded. "Darling Thieves," she answered, turning her iPod off.

"Is that a minstrel?" he asked, the confusion on his face softening his features slightly.

"Um, it's a group," she offered, not entirely understanding the question.

"A group of minstrels?" he asked again. "Or a group of thieves?"

She laughed at his joke, though he didn't laugh with her. "I'm Jewel," she said, hoping he would offer his name.

Instead, he asked out of nowhere, "You are friends with the boy called Kane, are you not?"

She felt her previously forgotten sadness come rushing back. There was no way she could keep the bitterness out of her voice as she answered, "We were friends."

The boy smiled at her admission. "You are angry with him?"

"Why? Do you know him?" It was virtually impossible for him to know Kane without her having any knowledge of it.

"He's seeing—" the boy paused, choosing his words carefully. "—someone who was a friend of mine romantically." It was obvious from the way he uttered the last word that he loathed the situation as much as she did. Suddenly, things began to make sense.

Jewel made the connection instantly. "The guy with the shaggy hair and blue eyes?" Of course he would know Kane's stranger. All hot guys knew each other.

The boy nodded. "His name is Hawk," he clarified.

"Hawk," she muttered to herself. "Another hippie."

The boy stared at her without speaking for several seconds, prompting her to look up at him to see why. When he realized she was waiting for him to speak, he almost barked out, "I don't like him either. Hawk, that is."

Jewel sighed as she said, "Kane isn't my favorite person either." She was feeling depressed again but tried to cover it.

"Perhaps we could dislike them together," he offered.

The look of sincerity on his face was just too much for her, and she had to laugh. "You can sit down, you know," she said, gesturing at the chair.

He pulled it out and sat across from her. "I'm serious, we are better than the way they treat us. I know you feel the same way."

She couldn't deny that. "I know, but what can we do about it?" she said, looking down in sadness.

"Figure out a way to get them back," he answered bluntly. When she looked back up to him she saw the same wolfish smile had returned to his face. "My name is Spike," he said, shoving his hand across the table. "We should become allies."

Jewel took his hand, not knowing where the hot new guy had come from, but as his eyes flashed with purpose, she realized he was making a certain amount of sense.

"SO EXPLAIN it to me," Kane said after Wanda had brought them their food.

Hawk scrutinized the plate in front of him with intensity. "There is a process that is complicated and involved," he said, not looking up. "These are not eggs," he added, looking back at Kane.

"Vegan. Egg substitute." Which was an explanation that did nothing to ease Hawk's mistrust of the food. "So try to summarize it, what's it consist of?"

The prince picked at the odd yellow substance with his fork as he explained. "It starts with the symmetry of facial features. The most attractive people have virtually identical placement of features on either side of their face." He looked up again. "How do you substitute an egg?"

"I never asked," Kane answered honestly. "So then it is all about looks?"

Hawk looked at the rack of condiments that sat on the table. With great deliberation he picked up the saltshaker and tried to smell its contents. "No. The process begins with looks. The Rite of Ascension is grueling, physical perfection is but one of the qualifications. Not many can survive it. This is like salt, correct?"

Kane nodded. "It *is* salt. So then what, there is a talent and swimsuit competition too?"

Hawk looked up, confused. "Swimsuit? What are you talking about? And this is not salt. It is smaller and smells of chemicals."

Kane took the shaker and smelled it himself. "I don't smell anything." He sprinkled some on his hand and licked it. "It's salt."

"There is no such thing as processed salt in Faerth," Ruber explained in the human's ear. "When used, it is sea salt and is pure."

"Okay then, this isn't your salt," Kane said, putting it down. He looked at the rack as well and grabbed the ketchup bottle. "Here, taste this," he said, handing it over.

Hawk opened the bottle and poked a finger inside and tasted it carefully. His eyes grew wide as he smiled. "What is *this*?"

"Um... sugared tomatoes, I think," Kane answered, bemused to see anyone that excited by ketchup. "So, what else then?"

Hawk practically drowned the egg substitute in a pool of ketchup and began to scoop forkfuls into his mouth. Through bites he said, "There are tests of wisdom, purity, and valor that must be passed, and then there is the challenge of mortality."

Kane began to choke on his food. He swallowed a huge gulp of water as he struggled to breathe again. In a wetly exasperated voice he asked, "Mortality? They try to kill them?"

Hawk shook his head no and looked over at the mustard bottle. "Not try, they do kill candidates. Is the yellow as good?"

"They *kill* you?" Kane exploded.

Hawk grabbed the bottle and sniffed it. "Yes, to see how you handle your last moments. Anyone who fears death is obviously not fit to rule." He dabbed a drop of mustard on his tongue and reared back in surprise. "That is not as good!" he said, grabbing his own water.

"They kill you?" Kane asked again, this time in utter and complete disbelief.

Hawk put the mustard down and pushed it away. "It is the final test. The Casters stop your heart. If you are filled with fear, then the spell is permanent, if you are accepting, you come back. What does BBQ stand for?"

Kane pushed it over to him. "You'll like it. But if you know you are coming back, why be afraid?"

Hawk sniffed the new bottle. "Because there is no certainty; there is always room for error when The Arts are concerned." He tasted the sauce and obviously loved it as he poured a good helping over the ketchup. "It's like the catch hup but with bite!" he exclaimed.

"So then you don't know if you will actually die?"

Hawk said with a full mouth, "No one knows that, hence the test."

Kane realized he had lost his appetite and pushed his plate away.

"You going to finish that?" Hawk asked hopefully.

Kane said nothing as he watched Hawk consume both breakfasts.

ON THE outskirts of town, where the weeds grew tall and wild, a foul wind swirled and snapped at old leaves and pieces of trash. The storm had receded, leaving overcast skies and a damp Athens in its wake. However, the tension that had accompanied the earlier weather hadn't disappeared. It seemed as if the weather had paused, taking a deep breath before its next stretch of explosive behavior. Mindlessly, the wind blew, and tall reeds bent aside, exposing a circle of grass that had been burned away and left behind charred earth.

This was the odd moment, between storm and sunlight, an artificial twilight between darkness and sun that was unsettled enough for magic to mold it to its bidding.

Though there was not a person left alive on the planet able to detect it, the area was saturated with arcane energies, remains left by Hawk and Spike's cross over. Intricate designs had been burned into the stems of grass and reed when they arrived. However, the detail had been washed away by the rain.

If there had been anyone present in the area, they would have seen new markings burning themselves into the ground. Steam rose from the damp grass before it was superheated and scorched as if by enormous heat.

A slow circle appeared, drawn out in ash and burned debris, looking exactly as if someone stood in the center, drawing a sigil with the point of a superheated stick. When the circle was completed, smaller, more detailed runes burnt themselves into the center. A brief pause followed the last stroke to the last rune, and the air itself began to shimmer with heat. A silent burst of light exploded silently from nowhere, and where there had been nothing but an empty field, there now stood three humanoid forms clad in dark leather armor.

Their faces were sharp featured, eyebrows and ears drawn upward to a point, the first indication they were in no way human. The second would be the stark whiteness of their hair in comparison to the cobalt-navy blue hue of their skin. When the clouds closed up and the sun was concealed, their skin looked more black than blue. However, no one seeing them would be taken in for a second. They each possessed two blades sheathed at their sides. Additionally, each possessed numerous smaller weapons hidden in various pockets in their clothing. The hidden armament was visible only briefly while they checked to ensure that everything had survived the cross over.

The tallest one stood in the center of the circle and surveyed their surroundings with unbridled disgust. In a language not heard on the world in over a thousand years he said to the others, "It stinks here, that will make tracking harder."

The one on his right seemed to chuckle, if that was what the clipped sound was meant to be. "Why bother? We know where the whelp is, we flush him out and kill him."

The leader shot his subordinate a withering glare. "Because there are about two hundred and sixty-two different accords saying we shouldn't even be here much less taking offensive action." He was gratified to see the lesser man look away in shame. "No, this is not a simple job. We are to retrieve Prince Hawk without raising suspicion or revealing our presence."

"Retrieve or kill?" the younger man asked.

The leader ignored the question since he wasn't sure what the answer was himself.

"If the prince refuses to hand it over?" his Second asked the leader.

"I am not convinced the boy needs to die yet," he answered after brief thought.

"And the Changeling?" the other man asked in a voice barely above a whisper.

The leader shrugged indifferently. "If he interferes we can kill him. We need a base of operations and then we need to find Spike, in that order." Both men nodded as they digested their orders.

Without another word, but clearly with a purpose, acting as a unit, they made for Athens, Iowa.

"SO THEN it isn't all about looks," I asked, after watching Hawk devour both plates along with four slices of toast and a bowl of fruit.

"Not all, but the better looking one is the better chance they have of being chosen for the ascension. Therefore, the better looking you are, the more status you possess."

I was still fuzzy on the specifics. "But why would looks even enter into it?"

Hawk shrugged. "The vessel of ascension has always been those that were the most comely. If there was a reason, it has been lost in time. Now it is a matter of tradition."

He answered so matter-of-factly that it sounded almost normal. There was much more to it than just looks, but I couldn't grasp it. "It sounds complicated." I had to admit.

He nodded, and I tried not to get lost in the way his bangs moved and covered his eyes. "What is your system based on? Money? Financial security? The professor at your academy didn't get around to explaining that yet."

"Um... we vote. I mean... well...." And I hated the words as I said them. "It's based on popularity."

I saw Hawk choke slightly on his water as he reacted to my explanation. "Popularity? I don't understand, you mean popular based on the most qualified, yes?"

I shook my head and tried not to think of the Governator. "No, just popular."

He rolled his eyes as he finished his drink. "And our way is shallow."

"He took that one, too, I believe," Ruber said as I tried not to complain out loud.

CHAPTER THIRTEEN

THE elderly human opened her door.

She barely had time to react to the three dark elves on her doorstep before the smallest of the three reached forward and snapped her neck. She didn't even have time to make a sound. Acerbus killed her in one movement.

"What are you doing!" Ater demanded, his furious tone freezing Acerbus in place.

"Eliminating the witness?" the Third answered, obvious fear lacing his voice.

"She is—was—useless!" Ater answered, kicking the man to accentuate his point. "Why would you even bother?" The youngest of their team had no answer as Ater snarled, "You are supposed to be one of the most fearsome killers in the nine realms! Are you telling me this human was a threat?" Of course, Acerbus had no answer. "We kill because we are ordered or are threatened. Explain to me what category she fell into?"

A hand clamped on his shoulder, the voice of his Second barely audible behind him. "Composure. You're showing emotion."

Ater knew his old friend was right and forced his emotions down. He had been a hired killer for almost four centuries, and this was only the fourth time he had ever cracked like this on a job. He took several seconds to compose himself before addressing the youngest of their party. "We are violating nearly every single accord in existence just by being here. By simply breathing this air we can be put to death," he explained in a patient voice. "Murdering innocents is not going to make our job any easier."

Acerbus rose to his feet slowly. He was unsure if these mood swings were normal for his new squad leader, but he did know he didn't like it. "Apologies, First," he offered weakly. "I assumed this was a standard mission."

"This is anything but," Ater countered, stepping over the human corpse as he entered the poor excuse of a house. "Dispose of that before it starts to smell and draws attention." Nose wrinkling in disgust at the dirt and the smells, he looked around the small house they had found on the outskirts of town.

The other two elves dragged the body into the house and closed the door behind them.

The house was claustrophobically small, but the hovel was still serviceable. Using it as a base, they could scout the town and learn the lay of the land. From here they could find the shape shifter and, through him, locate the prince.

The box in the corner made an annoying sound while strange images danced across—no, Ater realized, just under, its surface. All three elves stared at it, confused, their almond-shaped eyes unblinking. Music streamed out as a couple danced, and Ater saw Acerbus begin to sway in place. It was always like this with the younger ones. Those that were less than a century old or simply not trained would fall into a stupor in the face of Music, melodies making them almost zombies while they were played.

"I am tempted to let him stand there until he starves," Ater said to Pullus, the slightest tinge of amusement in his voice.

"It would make the rest of the mission a great deal quieter," the Second answered.

They both laughed as they watched the young elf drool with his mouth open. Ater sighed as he took a step toward the magic box. "There are times I miss being that young." The First drew his sword and, his motion a blur of speed, sliced the television in half. Sparks flew as glass exploded across the room. Acerbus flinched as the speaker squealed in complaint before dying completely. He shook his head, not sure how much time had passed.

Ater sheathed his sword and glared back at his Third. "The human isn't going to bury herself!"

He was gratified to see him jump into action instantly.

AFTER I paid for breakfast, we began to walk the streets of Athens.

The streets were still damp. The storm had receded for a while, but the air smelled of damp concrete, and the streets ran slick with watery oil washed out by the rain. In the sunlight, the wetter spots were almost iridescent.

Hawk seemed fascinated by the effect and wanted to know the cause. "Oil," I explained, trying not to be depressed that even in Hippieville we still suffered from pollution. "The cars—you know what a car is right?"

He gave me a look. "The clockwork carriages? I am not a child," he scoffed, although his voice held no sarcasm.

"So you have cars in your world?" I asked with a heavy dose of skepticism.

"They are not common, but there are certain beings that make such contraptions. There are tinkerers in Evna that make much more complicated devices than your kars," he boasted, his accent making the word *cars* seem foreign.

"Cars," I corrected him, and saw him repeat the word a few times under his breath. "Okay, so the cars use oil, and some of the oil ends up on the road. The water brings it to the surface of the pavement during wet weather. Together they make that effect." I pointed to a puddle of rainbow-jeweled water.

He smiled and nodded. "You mean the London effect."

I stopped. "London? As in the city?"

He stopped and looked back at me. "No, the London effect, where two objects that do not fit together are forced toward each other, producing an unexpected outcome."

I shook my head. "I don't understand."

He looked up as he tried to find the right words to explain. "When two things, like—Ruber, some assistance."

Ruber answered immediately. "Oil and water."

Hawk nodded. "Exactly. Like oil and water, or smoke and spirits. When the two are put together, they do not mix but instead produce an unexpected outcome."

"Smoke and…." I started to ask. And then thought better of it. "Never mind. But yes, oil and water is what is causing that iridescence."

"It's beautiful," he said, crouching down and touching the water as it rushed toward the gutter.

"It's really just pollution." He looked back in confusion, obviously not knowing the word. "Um, trash? Unclean residue?" Damn, I'd never had to think of what pollution meant before.

He looked back at the road and then to me with a huge smile. "Regardless of its origin, it is beautiful." After a second he added, "Like you."

I blushed as I tried not to think hard on the fact that he just compared me to pollution.

He stood up and wiped his hands off on his pants. "So you must have more questions. Let's hear them."

We began walking again, side by side, a little closer than two guys normally walked. "Why did you guys come here, of all places?"

"You mean the town?" he asked. I nodded, not sure what else he could be talking about. "To be honest, we didn't even know there was a town here, we just knew this was one of the few places of facilitation left on your world. The fact that Athens was here was, I assumed, providence."

"I thought you said Avalon was the only facilitate place here."

He smiled, and I knew I had obviously butchered the word. "There are two types of facilitation: bound and unbound. When the world is bound, transition requires no more effort than crossing a room. There is no magic or spell needed. To move to a world that has been abandoned or to a place without a facilitation point takes a bit more effort." The nonchalance he showed when he spoke about walking between worlds transfixed me. "You can move during the Blue hour, which is the safe way, or you can rip a hole through, but only at thin spots between the worlds."

"Athens is a thin spot then?" I asked, wondering what *thin* meant.

He nodded as we kept walking. "The area around it is. It is one of the few places on your world where magic still exists. A minor amount but it is here, nonetheless. At first I assumed it is a convergence of ley lines, but the fact that your town is built almost on top of it makes me wonder."

I stopped again. "There's magic in Athens?" I asked.

He paused as well. "Of course, did you think I could perform combat magic without it?"

He told me that as if he was asking how could you swim without water, yet I still had no clue what he meant. "There's no magic in Athens; it's just weird," I insisted.

His smile would have been so annoying on anyone else, all arrogant and condescending, but instead he just came off as amused. "So you're an expert on magic now?"

"No! I am just saying I've lived here all my life and never saw anything magical."

"And if you saw it, would you know what it looks like?" he asked good-naturedly.

I made a face and began walking again. "Shut up."

He laughed and pulled me back by my arm. I spun around in surprise as he gentled me into an embrace. "You are irresistible when you're angry," he said, his nose almost touching mine.

"We're on the street," I said in a whisper.

"And?"

"People can see us?" I protested.

His smile grew wider as he said, "Let them see, jealousy is good for the soul."

I had an answer to that, but his kiss interrupted my train of thought.

HE KISSES the boy and feels their passions join.

The bond that seems to connect them startles the young prince but he gives no outward sign. It reminds him of what tales of The Calling described.

He had heard those stories since the early childhood. Two people are drawn to each other and overcome great obstacles in order to do that. He'd liked them, especially the battle parts. As he had matured, he dismissed them as fables told to lull small children to sleep. But Hawk never forgot them. Each of the tales started in nearly identical fashion: when the universe came to be, there was one great soul of the universe, a living, breathing thing that lived and moved inside, as one. When the Creator began to shape the multitudes of worlds, she cut pieces of the soul up and used them to create all of life.

Through these souls, all life is connected. Hawk had liked that part of the tale, and, as had many others, translated it to mean that inside of each of us was a small piece of the Infinite, a shard of creation burning in each of our hearts.

In the stories, a Caster says that it is through this Infinite one that Hawk's people were able to access the magical forces that surround us all. The Aware can tap the magic. But among the Aware, only a very few have had the ability to harness the invisible power.

Fewer still, are those to whom Calling came.

When two pieces of the soul that had once been whole in the great tapestry met, they were irrevocably drawn to each other, becoming one soul residing in two bodies. There was no greater connection than the Calling, and over the centuries, many people had claimed to have experienced it. Hawk had simply assumed these people were using the age-old tales as an excuse for their sudden and drastic obsession for romantic love.

He had never thought Calling possible. But here he was, drawn to this boy and feeling the unmistakable echoing of emotions that bordered on empathic. The hollow ache of separation, the feeling of wholeness when they kissed. Hawk couldn't ignore what was happening and everything he's experiencing.

The problem was that Kane was human.

The story also states that each world was made of the same parts of the soul, meaning the Connection could only be made with one of your own people. There was great debate about this distinction, some claiming it was a social means of justifying xenophobic behavior, while others said that the Creator would never put one's soul mate out of their reach. Either way, it was generally agreed on that though people from other worlds could fall in love, The Calling was only for one of your own kind.

Yet here Hawk was with a human.

"You okay?"

Hawk blinked a few times, realizing his mind had wandered at some point during the kiss.

"Of course," he answered, flashing the boy a smile. "You take my breath away." Which was true, but had nothing to do with his lack of attention.

Normally Kane would blush and smile back, but from the way his eyes narrowed at Hawk's words it was obvious he didn't believe the sentiment behind them. "What's wrong?"

The list of things that were wrong at that moment staggered the young prince, but enumerating them wasn't what the human was looking for. Instead Hawk asked, "Explain to me again why we are not going to the academy."

Kane continued to stare at him for several seconds before he decided to answer. "It's Saturday, and it's called school, and you're changing the subject."

"So we go tomorrow, and yes I am," Hawk replied, smiling.

"No, we go Monday, and that's if they have school at all because of the fire." Kane's open annoyance was obvious, but Hawk let it slide for the moment. "Something like that doesn't just go away."

"So we have two days before we are expected anywhere?" The prince was trying not to think of the repercussions of their battle but it was hard. Kane nodded slowly with a confused look on his face. "I need to get back into the theater."

If the human's eyes could have fallen out of his head, they would have at that exact moment. "Are you insane!" Kane hissed, grabbing Hawk's arm and pulling him off the street. They stood in the space between Stop! Hammer Time, Mr. Trevor's hardware store, and There is a Flower Within My Heart, Ms. Coti's flower shop. Gritting his teeth in his effort to remain calm, Kane explained, "It's bad enough you had Spike start that damn fire, but they are going to be looking to see if it was arson or not. What do you think they are going to say if we're caught poking around?"

Hawk stared at him for a few seconds, waiting to see if there was any more to the question. When it was obvious there wasn't he tried answering. "I'm not sure, but I would assume they would start with some kind of exclamation. Then they'd ask us what we were doing there. By the way, who are 'they'?"

Now it was Kane's turn to pause in case there was more. "They are the police and the fire marshal. Hawk, I wasn't being literal. They will suspect us of having had something to do with it."

"We did." Hawk wasn't sure what the problem was, but whatever it was, Kane was obviously upset by it. "I need to test to see what kind of magic was used to animate the uniforms. It will tell me if there are Dark agents here or if it was something else."

"Something else?" Kane practically yelled. A couple walking by looked at them, and Kane smiled and waved as they walked by.

"Something else?" he asked in a lower voice. "What else could it be?"

Hawk shrugged. "I don't know with any certainty. There are several different possibilities that make sense. The Crimson Matriarch could have done it, but she'd never bother with something as minor as moving clothes." He sighed as he shook his head. "All of this is idle speculation until I can actually examine the site."

Hawk felt the tension of the situation begin to descend on him again and closed his eyes to steady himself. What he had told the boy was the truth, but not all of the truth. He had a very good idea who was responsible for the attack in the auditorium; he just didn't want to admit it to Kane or himself yet.

He felt Kane's hand on his shoulder. When he opened his eyes he saw the boy's eyes brimming with emotion. "Okay, we check out the theater. We just have to be careful."

Hawk smiled and pulled Kane into an embrace. This time Kane didn't complain that someone might see them.

CHARMING the girl had been disgustingly simple.

Spike had been taught the Art by his father and had found he possessed a knack for it. From time to time, he was even able to Charm the prince. The Changeling had been attempting to force the human to lose his interest in Hawk since their paths had intersected, but with no luck at all. Spike worried that humans in general might be immune to Charms but that fear evaporated once it held Jewel in thrall.

It had believed it would have to find a way to seduce her into betraying her friend, but it became obvious that she had no defense from his abilities. He quickly abandoned his plans to convince her and moved directly into controlling her every thought. He had commanded her to lead him to her house while it tried to figure a way to have revenge on Hawk while simultaneously saving the prince's—and its own—life from his father's wrath.

Spike was surprised to find her parents home.

Neither Hawk nor Spike had understood the complexities of what the humans called a "workweek," so the concept of a weekend was lost on the shape shifter. The girl's sire was heavier and flabbier than the daughter, but one source of her girth became evident at once. The sire was visibly confused by the fact of his, at best, average-looking daughter standing at the door with an especially handsome boy. However, his confusion lasted only for a moment.

Less than half a second passed, and Spike stole the man's mind and commanded him back into the house.

The three of them walked into the house, Spike closing the door behind them. He commanded the father to call the mother in, and within a matter of minutes he controlled the whole family. If all humans were this easily managed, it might have found a way to make this world livable. Quickly, it had the mother begin cooking him food, while it had the sire adjust the magical box Jewel called the teevee.

"So, Jewel," Spike said with a lazy leer, "how do we get Kane and Hawk for abandoning us?"

Her vacant eyes didn't even blink as she responded, "We can get Kane arrested. Put in prison."

Spike leaned forward. "Go on."

THE rain had reduced the remains of the theater to a soggy, mostly anonymous, pile of ash and scraps. Everything smelled gross.

Yellow tape closed off the area, but I didn't see anyone standing around. That was good since I had no idea how to explain our presence to a security guard. I nodded to Hawk that the area was clear and took a step to cross the street, but he stopped me.

"What are the bindings for?" he asked, gesturing at the tape.

"It says it's a crime scene," I explained, but he just gave me that familiar blank stare. "It's forbidden to cross because they are investigating it?" I tried.

"What happens if we cross it?" His voice was deep with suspicion.

"Um, we get in trouble if caught?"

He looked at me as if I was insane. "That's it?"

I nodded. "That's pretty much what most of the signs mean." I had a feeling things were much worse on his world. "Why? What should happen?"

He shook his head angrily as he crossed the street. "I don't understand this world at all. How do leaders maintain order if breaking a law has no consequences?"

I followed him, watching everywhere, making sure I hadn't missed anyone. "There are tons of consequences if we get caught!"

"It is a bit late by that time, don't you think?" he called back as he began to make his way through the ash-covered debris. "It seems to me that if you had some form of punishment immediately it might be more effective since escaping detection looks as if it's painfully simple."

"I have a feeling I don't want to break a law in your world," I said. He paused and looked back at me with a grave expression on his face. "No. You'd don't." I decided not to press the point. I followed his steps toward the spot where the stage had once stood.

I wasn't sure what he was looking for. Everything looked like a grayish black, melted, soot-covered, moldy-paper-and-cloth mess to me. From the way he poked methodically through the mess with the tip of his boot, he was on the hunt for something specific.

I felt completely exposed; we stood out in the open with no place to hide if shit went down. If Hawk was the least bit concerned, he didn't show it. For a second, I considered being pissed off, however, freaked out won. "Can we hurry this up?" I asked after a few minutes. "I have a bad feeling about this."

He knelt down, brushing a lump of soaked wood aside. At once, his body froze in place; I looked at him and saw from his expression that he found what he was looking for. "Ruber, some assistance, please."

"Is that acceptable?" the gem asked me in my ear.

"If it gets us out of here quicker? Please," I replied softly.

I felt the gem wiggle out of my ear and watched it expand in size as it floated toward Hawk. Hawk pointed at something lying unburned beneath the debris and sighed. "See what you can detect there." A flickering light appeared under the ruby, emanating down to the area Hawk had dug out. "There are traces of arcane energies… they are Arcadian in origin." The lights began to quicken. "I can sense—"

"*Freeze!*" a voice called out behind us.

I spun around and saw two policemen standing on the edge of the fire. "Kane Vess?" one of them called out. I nodded, panicked, not sure if I should raise my hands or not. "Come on out of there, we have some questions for you." I looked over my shoulder and wasn't that surprised to not see Ruber or Hawk. I turned around slowly and raised my hands, wondering exactly when it was his life had become such a tub of crap.

HAWK and Ruber crouched behind the field of invisibility, watching the police put Kane into the police car.

"That can't be good," Hawk said quietly.

"I believe that is the very definition of not good," Ruber agreed.

CHAPTER FOURTEEN

JEWEL hung up the phone and sat on the couch quietly.

"Well done," Spike said as it shoved an entire leg of turkey in his mouth and pulled out a bone. "So he will be incarcerated?"

Jewel nodded blankly. "He's arrested."

Spike could see the emotion moving silently behind her eyes. She was distressed beyond measure, but his control over her mind was absolute. "And they will what? Kill him?"

He saw her expression drop in horror at the same instant that her emotions freed her from Spike's magic before he could regain control over her again. "No," she said, her body shaking from the stress. "They will try to prove he set the fire and then call his dad." Again, he felt the panic rise and the hold on her mind slip, but he bore down and forced her to obey. "He will be in a lot of trouble," she finally decided on.

"Trouble is good," Spike said to himself as he leaned back and began to devour another piece of turkey.

A voice said from behind him, "Not all trouble." There was a small prick in his back, and Spike felt his world grow dark. His last thought was only one word.

Assassins.

KANE knew he was screwed.

He had never been in trouble before, but he was pretty sure this was the most trouble you could be in and not be legally shot. He sat in the interview room wondering what was taking them so long? They had caught him dead to rights at the scene of the crime. He was pretty sure that made him a criminal. How much more did they need?

And then it hit him. The police or the school were probably trying to call his dad.

The thought that he couldn't feel any worse was quickly dispelled and replaced with the thought that this was just the tip of the feeling-crappy iceberg. He felt himself sliding further down in his chair, wishing he was dead. The buzz of the fluorescent lights was deafening in the small room as Kane waited for his life to end.

An older policeman entered the room after long, agonizing minutes. He held a folder in one hand and had a box in his other. He studied the contents of the folder and, without looking up, placed the box between them and sat across from Kane. "Kane Vess, sophomore at Qunice and taking drama." He closed the folder and looked directly at the younger man. "So you wanna tell me why you burned the theater down?"

Kane felt his mouth go dry as his heart seemed to stop beating. It was at that moment he realized he would never be a career criminal. "I, um… I didn't?" he said, but with his voice cracking from stress it came out as a question.

"Oh, you did," the cop said, leaning forward. "What I want to know is why?"

Kane tried to swallow and realized his tongue felt like he had just trekked across the desert in search of whatever it was people looked for in the desert. "Can I get some water?" he asked in a croak.

"Sure," the man said, smiling. "As soon as you tell me why you burned down the theater."

Kane had no idea what to say to that. He opted for denial. "I didn't," he said more forcefully.

"So then you can explain why you were poking around a crime scene?"

Kane knew he couldn't. "I was just looking around." The words sounded lame to him, he couldn't imagine how it sounded to the cop.

"Looking for this?" he said, opening the box.

Kane looked at the half-charred remains of his backpack. It was covered in black soot, and part of it was burnt away, but it was unmistakably his. He tried to swallow again and said in a weak voice, "That's not mine?"

"The fire department had found a small amount of stuff that wasn't completely engulfed. We had no idea whose this was until a witness came forward today and said you claimed to be in the theater before it caught fire." He put the cover back on the box. "So let's start over," he said with an overly large smile. "Why did you burn down the theater?"

Kane felt like he was going to cry as he opened his mouth even though he had no idea what he was going to say.

Before he had to decide, the door opened again and both of them looked over and saw Hawk walk in. The officer stood up, obviously upset. "This is an interrogation, you can't just walk in here like…," he began to roar, but Hawk locked eyes with the older man and said in a low tone. "Sit down and be quiet."

The policeman sat down instantly. The look on his face made it clear he was as shocked as Kane was by the action. Hawk closed the door behind him and sat next to Kane. "Sorry it took so long, it took Ruber some time to figure out where they'd take you."

The ruby floated up, expanding to its full size. "That is untrue," it said in that same distant cousin-to-a-British accent. "He had no idea where you'd been taken; it just took him some time before he asked me for directions."

The cop's eyes bulged out at the talking, floating ruby. Exasperated, he grunted and glared at the boys and the gem.

"What are you doing here?" Kane asked, trying to ignore the man.

"Rescuing you, of course," Hawk answered with a smile. "You didn't expect me to allow them to take you?"

"This is you rescuing me?" Kane said, pointing to the police officer, whose face was now red with shock. "You ever hear of stealth?"

Hawk gave him that all-knowing grin and said, "You ever hear of The Charms?"

Kane had to admit he hadn't.

"Watch," Hawk said, turning to the cop. "Kane did not start that fire."

The man's face relaxed as he stared forward as if drunk. "Kane did not start the fire," he repeated.

"In fact, he had nothing to do with the fire at all."

The man's face twisted in confusion as he tried to digest the new and forcefully stated idea. "He-he did have… something…."

The prince furrowed his brow in concentration as he said again, "He had nothing to do with the fire at all."

The older man's body began to shake as if he was having a stroke. "But… he… did…."

"He is resisting," Ruber commented, pointing out the obvious.

"Thank you for that," Hawk said acidly.

"What are you doing?" Kane asked, confused and horrified.

"The same thing I tried on you the first time we talked," Hawk said, sighing with weariness. Seeing the officer's distress, he commanded, "Sleep." The man's head fell forward to the desktop immediately.

"Fairies are able to charm individuals with lesser wills," Ruber began to explain. "Think of it as an instant form of hypnotism."

"You tried to mind wipe me?" Kane asked, his voice growing louder in shock.

"Of course I did!" Hawk snapped back. "You had seen me, were somehow immune to the magic of my blade, and I had no idea why. What in the Dark did you expect me to do?"

Kane tried to calm down, realizing he was more upset by the circumstances than at Hawk himself. "So then why isn't it working on him? Maybe it wasn't me?"

"You're insinuating I am lacking in my Talents?" Hawk asked, giving him a dark look.

Kane ignored it. "Don't start getting all princey on me! You just broke into a police station, and I'm still in trouble!"

"Perhaps the key word is hypnotized," Ruber said, floating to the other side of the table and hovering over the file.

Both boys looked at the gem and called out, "What?"

Ruber's voice became even more controlled as he explained, "As I was explaining to Kane, The Charm is nothing more than hypnotism, simply an accelerated version of it."

Hawk shook his head and practically snarled, "That word means nothing to me."

"You mean he can't make him do something he wouldn't normally do," Kane answered, ignoring Hawk's outburst.

"Exactly. Those who are formally skilled in The Charms are indeed able to sway a person's mind into thoughts and actions they normally wouldn't perform, but Hawk here is not so skilled." As Ruber had talked, the folder's cover had floated open, and the papers inside flipped over as if blown by a gentle wind.

"Thank you for pointing out my shortcomings," Hawk muttered under his breath.

"You're welcome, but that was not my intent," Ruber replied, sounding distracted. "I believe you are trying to make this man do something he would normally never do."

"And what is that?" Hawk demanded.

"According to this report, the reason the police were looking for Kane in the first place was because a witness came forward stating that they had heard him saying he was in the theater before the fire."

"You told someone?" Hawk asked, incredulity lacing his words.

"No!" Kane said loudly. "No," he said again, this time softer. "No!" he said a third time, this time in realization. He looked at Hawk, his eyes wide in disbelief. "Jewel!"

Hawk didn't seem to understand for a second and then he got it. "The girl!"

"And her boyfriend," Ruber added.

Kane turned to the ruby and exclaimed in protest, "Jewel doesn't have a boyfriend!"

"Well it seems she does now," the gem said ominously. "A boyfriend named Spike."

"Oh fornication!" Hawk said darkly.

SPIKE woke slowly. Once the fog in his mind cleared, it tried to move and realized he could feel nothing from the neck down.

He looked up and was not the least surprised to find himself staring into the cold eyes of a dark elf. He forced down the panic forming in his gullet and stated in the calmest voice he could muster, "My father sent you."

Ater nodded as he stepped back a pace, a poison-laced dagger still in his hand. "You don't look surprised."

Spike sighed as he tried to shift his body even a little, but he knew the assassins were more than skilled at dealing with his kind. "He said he would give me seven days."

"He lied," Ater said, watching his men cart the unconscious human forms upstairs. Once they were gone, he knelt back down to make eye contact with the shape shifter. "Using Charms against untrained beings. That's punishable by death. Escaping to an abandoned world. That's punishable by death. Making exodus from a world with unregulated artifacts. That's a death sentence for each item taken. You aren't having a good season, Changeling."

"An assassination attempt on an abandoned world. That's a death sentence. Harming a royal guardian. That's a death sentence. Making a hostile move against an heir to the throne. That's a death sentence." Spike smiled up at Ater, showing all this teeth. "How many times can they kill us anyways?"

Ater placed the tip of the knife under Spike's chin. "I am thinking one is more than enough." Spike closed his mouth when he saw the deadly intent in the elf's eyes. "Fortunately for you, I am in the middle of what seems to be a moral quandary. So I am going to give you one chance to end this without anyone dying." Ater rolled the knife over his knuckles and caught it in mid flip. The sheer dexterity it took to perform the feat was not lost on Spike. "Your father wants the key to Ascension. The prince has it. Now, I don't want to kill the boy if possible, but the prince's fate rests on the path you choose next."

Spike didn't even see the blade move before he felt a sharp pang of pain explode in his neck. His body went from numb to overwhelming agony as every nerve ending came back to life. He screamed and rolled around on the floor as he clutched his sides, trying to ride the white-hot wave of pain that rolled through his body. Ater's voice cut through the haze that had descended on Spike's consciousness as if he was whispering in the Changeling's ear.

"You know what the key is. Go, get it, bring it to me. If you do this, I don't care what you and the boy do. My orders are to kill both of you, by the way." Spike froze at those words. "Your father's betrayal is far deeper than not giving you your time. Again, I am offering you a great kindness." His face was next to Spike's now. "Bring me the key or I will kill both of you. You have until the sun comes up."

Spike closed his eyes and waited for the inevitable physical punctuation at the end of the threat.

When he opened his eyes he was alone in the house.

The clock had just started to count down for Spike.

"SHE'S in trouble!" I yelled, kicking the chair out from under me as I stood up.

Hawk's hand closed around my wrist as he held me in place. "We are all in trouble. One problem at a time." His voice was annoyingly calm considering his pet shape shifter was out there with my best friend.

"If she gets hurt it is my fault!" I pleaded with him.

"No," he said in a soft voice. "It will be mine." Despite the danger, I could feel the sorrow radiate off of him like it was an open flame. "Ruber, what *can* we convince the officer about Kane?"

The lights under the floating ruby continued to flicker over the papers. "Well, according to the witnesses, they place him in the theater before it caught on fire. I would assume at the very least he would think Kane saw who started the fire."

"He wants to play games," I heard Hawk say under his breath, a dangerous tone entering his voice. "Then let us play games." He turned to the police officer, and from the look on his face, was concentrating on something. "You questioned Kane and were convinced beyond a shadow of a doubt he had nothing to do with the fire. He did see someone who resembled this Spike person who was questioned, and you think you should look closer into that."

Unlike the other commands, the cop seemed to accept what Hawk was saying. I tried not to feel sick about what we were doing.

"After I walk out of this room you will forget I was ever here and allow Kane to leave. Is that satisfactory?"

I saw the older man nod like a zombie and had to look away before I lost my lunch. Hawk seemed too casual about it, twisting the man's memories as if they were nothing. And he had wanted to do it to me! Hawk asked Ruber, "Anything else?"

"I believe that will do it." I could feel Hawk's gaze on me as the room grew silent.

"Kane," I heard him say.

I looked over at him and felt that same half a second of

exhilaration I had every time I laid eyes on him. He smiled, and I realized that he felt the same thing. "We are going to wait for you outside. As soon as you're free we will go see Jewel, okay?"

I nodded but knew if I tried to say anything I'd end up bawling.

He leaned down next to me, taking my hand between both of his and squeezing. "I know you didn't ask for any of this. I am truly sorry I brought this into your life." I felt a tear roll down my cheek as the mental dam that I had walled my emotions behind began to crack.

"I-it's just too much," I said, hating the way my voice cracked and made me sound like a wuss.

"I know," he said, leaning his head against mine. "And you're not a wuss."

I looked up quickly, knocking our heads together. "How did you—*ow!*" I shouted, rubbing my head.

He was doing the same with a grin on his face.

"How did you know what I was thinking?" I asked, albeit a bit more forceful than I intended.

"You were thinking that?" he asked, his smile dropping instantly.

"You called me a wuss, what does that even mean?" I asked, knowing there was no way the bauble could translate a word like wuss.

It was obvious he didn't know what it meant but he was just realizing what he had just said. He tried to cover it up quickly by saying, "I've heard you use it before." But we both knew I wasn't buying it.

He was losing it too. I wouldn't have noticed before, but as he got up and started giving orders I could see it in his eyes. "Ruber, stay with Kane, I will wait for you two outside." He began to walk to the door and looked back at me with a fake smile. "It's all right, I promise."

I didn't know who he was lying to, me or himself.

I saw Ruber float toward me, shrinking down as he slipped into my ear. Once the gem was in place, Hawk nodded to me and walked out the door.

"Just because you didn't do anything doesn't mean you aren't in trouble," the officer said out of nowhere. I turned around quickly, trying to piece together the imaginary conversation he thought we were in the middle of. "You should have come to us immediately." He looked down at the papers and frowned. "And you are sure you saw this Spike character in the theater as well?"

I nodded, not sure what words his mind had created for me to say.

"And this Jewel girl too?"

"No!" I half shouted. "I mean, she wasn't even there." I tried to cover quickly.

"Then why would she say she saw you in there if she wasn't with her boyfriend?"

I bit my bottom lip to stop myself from blurting out. "He isn't her boyfriend!" Instead, I said in the calmest voice I could muster, "She was scared he might get in trouble, I told her she could say she saw me instead."

It made no sense but then I was pretty sure that today would never make a lot of sense to him. "Well, I still need to find this boy. I will let the school know you weren't involved, but not coming forward wasn't right either."

"I'm sorry?" I offered.

He closed his eyes for a moment, his features clenching in pain for a second. "Just don't let it happen again," he said, obviously distracted. "Just go on, you can go."

I was unsure if I should leave him, since his pain was directly my fault but then I thought about Spike with Jewel and found the will to walk out. "I'm sorry, sir," I said honestly. He waved me off, and I walked out of the room.

It took everything I had not to sprint out of the police station.

HAWK stood outside the police station masking his presence from the few people who walked by. There was something in the air, a scent there, just a trace at about head height that made him anxious. He could see nothing out of place, but he knew he was being watched.

He looked up and saw Spike hanging upside down from the roof, looking down at him.

Hawk shifted his pack around so he could draw Truheart but realized he had left it at Kane's. Spike flipped down and held its empty hands out, pleading. "Wait, I beg you to listen."

Hawk said nothing, and they both knew the prince was reciting magical spells in his mind.

"The Dark are here, and they have been sent to kill you," Spike said quickly. "Your life is in danger."

"My life has been in danger longer than that," Hawk said as he continued to weave the combat magic around him.

"Listen!" Spike implored. "They just want the key, surrender it to them, and they'll let you live." The coldness that was reflected in Hawk's eyes was doubly chilling to the Changeling. "We have a chance to escape; they don't want to kill you."

Spike's gaze darted up and over Hawk's shoulder for a moment and then shifted back to the prince. "Just give them the key!" he hissed.

Hawk looked over his shoulder quickly but saw nothing at all. When he turned back he wasn't that shocked to find Spike no longer standing in front of him.

Hawk realized the clock had just started counting down on his time left in this realm as he turned back around and studied the skyline behind him.

"DOES he know we're here?" Pullus asked the First.

Ater shook his head and held his hand up to his Second for

silence. He was reasonably sure the prince had not spotted them, but he wasn't going to take any chances.

"Why don't we just kill them?" Acerbus asked.

Both dark elves shot the younger man a withering stare. The Third felt himself pull back from the glares, wondering if he was the one about to die.

When Ater looked back at the fairy, the youngling was staring across the street, searching too close to where they were concealed. He froze, knowing only a novice dropped down once spotted. Visual identification was registered in moving targets, if the boy was looking their way it was because he couldn't see anything. He cursed the elders once again for ordering him to lead this expedition as he waited for the damned noble to look away.

A human came bounding out of the structure, diverting the heir's attention immediately. Moving as one, the three assassins ducked down out of sight, crouching on the roof, waiting. Pullus put two fingers to his eyes and then gestured behind them, asking in the silent language of their people, "Did he see us?"

Ater's hands moved in a blur as he answered, "I don't think so, but if he did, I am killing that one." He pointed at Acerbus and made the universal slashing motion across his throat. The junior member of their trio flinched.

Ater and Pullus had been part of the same team for over three hundred years, trained killers for the Lords of Arcadia. Their Third had been lost in hostile action off world, and they had been forced to take on a new recruit to train.

So far, Ater had threatened to kill the new man sixteen times.

Pullus gestured, "I am going to check." Ater nodded as his hand tightened on his weapon. When the Dark revolted against the throne, the dark elves threw their allegiance behind their own kind, taking orders for the rebellion. Thus far, their action had been limited to gathering intelligence on Arcadia's defenses and determining how best to storm the capital. This was the first assassination they had been given since going rogue.

Ater knew he should have been concerned about the ease with which they had switched sides, but there was no time to think about it at the moment.

Pullus ducked back down and reported in whisper, "They're gone."

The three dark elves gave a sigh of relief as they readied themselves to move. "We've been over this. We cannot just kill him," the First said, spinning on Acerbus. "That boy has the secret to ascension on his person, and if we were to kill him, we wouldn't learn what that secret is, would we?" Acerbus shook his head silently, as Ater continued. "If you compromise our location again, you won't even know your head isn't connected to your body until it hits the ground. Are we clear?"

Acerbus swallowed hard and said, "As you command."

He could feel Pullus standing behind him, concerned. His Second knew that a rooftop in a strange world was not the place for explanations, but Ater was quickly losing patience for their mission and this world. He had never even heard of this realm a week ago. He had absolutely no working knowledge of the place since no one had been here in centuries. There were strict accords preventing incursions such as theirs into Abandoned worlds. The Changeling knew what he had been talking about as far as that went. The rules agreed on by the nine worlds were inviolate and meant to be abided by, yet here he was, breaking every one of them.

Again, he wished it hadn't been so damn easy to not care.

"Pullus, track the Changeling. We will follow the prince," Ater commanded, trying to calm his own inner turmoil. The Second nodded and bounded off the roof without a second's hesitation. Ater double-checked that his blades were secured before turning to follow. "Keep up. If you're seen, you're dead," he informed Acerbus before leaping after Pullus.

CHAPTER FIFTEEN

HAWK stood waiting for me when I jogged out of the police station.

He looked like he was watching the stars from the way he was watching the skies. "C'mon!" I said, pulling him by the arm. "Jewel's in danger!" I felt some resistance; he was reluctant to move. I wasn't in the mood to ask what was wrong. Bad enough Hawk's insanity had invaded my world, but if Jewel got hurt because of me….

I banished the thoughts and opened my stride into a run, heading straight to her house.

Hawk kept pace with me since I knew the way, but his lack of conversation seemed odd. The silence wasn't what made me uneasy. I couldn't explain it, I took it as a sign of the dangerous situation we were walking into and began to run faster. The first word he said was a question. "Ruber?"

"Three, one advance scout, two following us," the gem confirmed almost instantly.

"Damnation." I heard Hawk mutter quietly, which made me slow up.

"What?" I asked, reading the first sign of real concern on his face. Most of the time he looked like he was my age in the way he carried himself. He smiled, joked, and generally seemed to be as normal as a guy from another world can be. But there were times like this when his features seemed to change. His eyes became darker, and it was like looking at someone ten years older than me.

He shook his head slightly and began to pull ahead of me. "Don't look behind us, and keep up."

It took every single bit of my patience not to look over my shoulder.

"Ruber, I need my weapons," he said, his voice barely audible to me.

"I shall return." I heard the gemling answer as he vanished from my ear.

"Are we in trouble?" I asked him, straining to keep up with his pace.

"Yes."

I felt the familiar tingle of fear begin to fill me. Half of me was glad that I was trusted enough to get the truth but the other half wished he didn't know we were being followed. As we turned the corner I could see the lights on in Jewel's house, music was blaring from the open front door. Hawk skidded to a halt, his face filled with apprehension. I stopped, not sure what the problem was. "Why are we stopping?"

He kept staring at the house. His eyes looked like they were frozen in a thousand-mile stare. "Music" was all he said.

"Music?" I repeated, not sure what he meant. He took a hesitant step forward. The action had none of the normal grace he possessed when moving. If anything, it looked like he was fighting himself.

"Music," he said again. "Can't resist—"

He took another step and then another. His movements were stiff and robotic; he really looked like he was being pulled against his will.

I stood in front of him, not sure what was wrong. I knew walking into the house unarmed and moving as awkwardly as a spaz wasn't a viable plan of action. "We aren't waiting for Ruber?" I asked as he kept walking at me. I expected him to look at me or at the very least stop walking. Instead, he pushed me aside with one hand, throwing me to the grass with embarrassingly little effort. "Hawk?" I called out, but he kept walking.

I had gathered myself to get up when Ruber appeared in front of me. Hawk's bag fell to the ground beneath him. "I brought your supplies as… oh my," was all the ruby said as it noticed Hawk wandering across Jewel's lawn.

"What's wrong with him?" I asked, my voice rising as my panic grew.

"Music," Ruber said darkly. "Fairies are exceedingly vulnerable to Music and its effects. The younger ones can become transfixed by it."

"Music?" I exclaimed. "He can fight like a ninja but Britney Spears is his kryptonite?" This made no sense to me.

"He is already under its sway," Ruber said as Hawk got closer and closer to the house. "We need to stop its source, but if Spike is in there…."

"…then this is probably a trap," I finished for him.

"Undoubtedly."

"I can't just let Hawk walk in there and let Spike kill him," I said, kneeling down, opening the pack.

"Yet there is no way for you to adequately defend yourself against the Changeling," Ruber said as I realized the only thing in the pack was Hawk's school materials. "Where is his sword?" I asked.

"It was in there before I left, there is an enchantment which conceals the bag's contents from anyone casually opening it."

I felt all around inside of it. "Well how do I get it out!" I asked as Hawk got closer and closer to the front door.

"The specifics were never shared with me."

Which was Ruber-speak for "I don't know."

"Screw it," I said, dropping the bag and running after Hawk. I had to do something. I had to save him, and I was going to have to do it by himself. I thought about tackling him, but if he struggled he would kick my ass in about three seconds. I had nothing that could physically stop him, but I couldn't let him just walk in into a trap.

As I got to him, I looked at his face and realized he was completely helpless. Suddenly I got an idea and slipped my hand into my pocket. When my fingers curled around my phone, I knew how to save him.

SPIKE liked the way the humans danced.

The girl had been as easily controlled a second time, which was a source of great amusement to it. Leading young fairy children astray with Music was an old-world trick. The practice had been outlawed for several centuries, and Spike had never been given the chance to indulge.

Making the girl dance endlessly for him was almost as fun.

Spike knew it was just a matter of time before Hawk found it. The prince was not going to listen to him, which meant Spike had to take the decision out of the young Faerth's hands. For Hawk, it was all about pride and honor, but to Spike, it was about survival. He knew his father would never rest; if he didn't get the key, nothing else mattered.

Puck could go jump off a cliff as far as Spike was concerned.

It was power that Puck craved, and it was power Spike would give him. Spike didn't really want Hawk dead, he wanted to be able to claim ascension without challenge, and Spike knew how to ensure that. He was the only being the prince had shared the secret of his family's power with, the true reason they had sent their son so far away. There were allies that they could have sent Hawk to, but none they could trust with the secret of their power.

Hawk stumbled into the doorway, his eyes were glazed over by the power of the Music, his mind a million miles away. Spike's face stretched into an inhuman grin, the edges of his mouth touching the sides of his face. He clapped his hands in glee as he moved toward the entranced noble. "Not so mighty now, are we?" Spike said, rising from the chair.

Jewel continued to prance around the living room; she was moving sluggishly and sweating badly. She had been dancing for more than twenty minutes as hard as she could, and no doubt her body was weak with such exertion. Spike didn't even give her a second glance as he stepped in front of Hawk. He clasped the prince's chin with his hand. "You are too beautiful to waste your time with these creatures," Spike declared, the desire in his eyes making him look crazed. "I will save our lives, and in time, you will learn to love me instead."

Hawk turned his gaze to Spike, the confusion completely gone. "I'm sorry, are you speaking to me?" Spike's eyes bulged in shock as Hawk's hand shot up and grasped the Changeling's neck. "You are playing a dangerous game, trickster," Hawk growled in fury.

"How?" Spike asked as he struggled to draw breath. The prince's grip was like steel, he could feel his head begin to swim from lack of air.

The Music stopped suddenly. Spike looked over and saw Kane holding the power cord for the music box. He nodded to Hawk who reached up to his ears and pulled out what looked like two white strings connected to two buds that had been nestled in his ears. Spike could hear the faint sound of a voice coming from them.

Hawk's smile was infuriating. "iPod."

Hawk threw Spike across the room. The Changeling slammed up against the wall, hard. Hawk pulled the sword out of the back of his belt and rushed at him with a dangerous look in his eyes. Kane screamed out to him. "She's still dancing!"

Hawk's grip adjusted in mid stride, he slapped Spike across his face with the flat of the blade, stunning the creature and throwing it to the side. "Release the human now," he ordered as Spike scrambled to his feet. "Let her go and earn mercy."

"Mercy?" Spike screamed. "You talk to me of mercy?" His human features melted like wax, revealing the creature underneath. "All I ever did was love you! What mercy did you show me then?"

Hawk paused, seemingly stunned by the words. "Love?" Spike paused as well, waiting for some kind of declaration from the prince. "What does a monster like you know of love?"

The words hurt more than any weapon could.

"Monster!" Spike screeched. "You think me a monster! I protected you! I defended you! I'm trying to protect you now!"

"You enchanted the uniforms!" Hawk shot back. "The magic trace on them was of Faerth origin. Raw magic! The type your kind use."

"I was trying to scare the boy!" Spike attempted to explain. "He is a danger to you!"

"You Charmed me! Enchanted the man to kill us!" Hawk roared, bringing the sword up for attack. "What kind of love is that?"

"The only kind that counts!" Spike called out as he dodged the lunging attack, retreating further into the house to escape the sword. "You aren't thinking clearly; the human has clouded your judgment."

Hawk sliced the air between them with a vicious swipe. "I think I'm seeing things clearly for the first time." His voice was dark with anger as Spike continued to retreat. "You care nothing for anyone but yourself! Use people as playthings with little to no regard for their life or dignity."

"Are we speaking of me or you?" Spike asked, his mocking grin causing Hawk to swing again. "When was the last time you cared for anyone that wasn't royalty?" he asked, ducking under the sword, moving back toward the dining room.

"You're killing that girl!" Hawk bellowed. "You're abusing the Charm for your own amusement!"

"And you used it to get your pet human out of jail," Spike countered. "How is that different?" Hawk said nothing as the words hit home. "Oh, did I get too close with that? You think me a monster but it is *your* people who have kept an entire civilization under the heel of your boot. Do you know what every race that is part of the Dark has in common?" Spike asked, but answered before Hawk could answer. "We are all hideous by your standards! Ugly serve while beauty rules. Would you have spurned me if I looked like this?"

Spike's visage changed into that of a perfect boy. His hair blond and fair, his eyes sparkled golden. He was everything that Hawk would have said he wanted less than a week ago. Yet as he looked at the Changeling all he could feel was revulsion.

"I'd still say you're a monster," Hawk said, his voice heavy with emotion.

"*Why!*" Spike screamed, his face melting back to his own.

"Because, only a monster forces themselves on those who refuse. It isn't the fact you're a monster, Spike, it's because you don't know the difference between love and obsession."

"Hawk!" Kane called out. "She is about to collapse!"

The momentary distraction was all Spike needed.

Extending his claws he climbed up the wall and over Hawk's head, flipping over as he rushed directly at Kane. "*It's your fault!*" the Changeling screamed as he leapt at him. Kane brought his hands up automatically as he closed his eyes in terror.

A spear plunged through Spike's chest, stopping his forward motion, dropping him to the ground.

Jewel fell to the rug like a puppet whose strings had been cut as Spike writhed on the floor, impaled on the weapon. Hawk and Kane looked over at the door and saw the three dark elves standing there, one of their hands extended from the throw.

"M-my lord…," he said, trying to reach toward Hawk with his arm.

In one moment all of the rage and anger Hawk had harbored toward the Changeling faded as he watched it die on the carpet. Hawk rushed to the Changeling's side, the wound was far too serious for anything to be done. "Puck… wants the key…," he gasped, struggling on each word.

Hawk nodded, trying to put his life-long friend at ease. "It's dealt with," he said, keeping one eye on the trio of assassins at the door.

"I'm... sorry...," he gasped as his eyes stopped glowing, going from bright gold to a dull yellow.

Seeing that Spike was gone, he lowered his friend's head to the floor and stood slowly. He glared at the dark elves, daring them to move. "You murdered him."

Ater nodded. "He was about to kill a human in cold blood. That is against the accords."

"You being here is against the damned accords!" Hawk screamed at them.

The dark elf didn't argue, he just sighed as he made a gesture with his hand. The spear shimmered and vanished from Spike's chest, appearing in his hand instantly. "There is enough innocent blood already spilt on his foolish mission, there doesn't need to be anymore." He locked eyes with Hawk, and in a much firmer tone said, "You know why we're here. Surrender the key to Ascension to us and this is over." The other two elves shifted their weight, readying for a fight.

"You're not here to kill me?" Hawk asked suspiciously, as he realized that Spike might not have been lying.

"I have been an assassin longer than you've been alive, boy, I've killed more people than you have ever spoken with, each one in defense of our world. I am not a thug who is sent to make a political statement. I am a killer only when it protects our realm. You are not a threat. Your family has committed endless atrocities that need to be answered for, but you are just a boy. Nothing is gained by killing you. Give me the key and vow never to return."

Hawk studied the elf's eyes for any signs of deception.

"You know I am not going to do that," Hawk said, tightening the grip on Truheart.

"If you are smart, you will," Ater said grimly.

"Hawk, what are they talking about?" Kane asked as the two adversaries stared at each other.

"Get ready to run," Hawk said, seeing the intent in the other men's posture.

"Make this a fight and the boy's life is forfeit," Acerbus said from behind Ater.

Ater's face tightened, but he didn't even blink as he watched the prince. "Shut up!" he said to the Third.

The younger elf seemed chastised for a moment and then a defiant look crossed his face. "No!" he called out, whipping his dagger up. "You are weak and jeopardizing the mission!" He threw the dagger directly at Kane, aiming for the point between his eyes.

Hawk moved as quickly as possible, trying to intercept the blade with his own and knock it out of the air.

His eyes widened as he missed.

The dagger hit at the point where his neck and shoulder met, throwing him back into Kane's arms.

Kane gaped down as Hawk looked up at him. "Run…," Hawk said as blood began to trickle down his neck.

Ater reacted instantly, he turned and swung his blade at Acerbus with practiced ease. The assassin's head separated from his shoulders without a sound. "I warned you," he said to the severed head. Turning to his Second he ordered, "Pullus, stabilize the prince, we are bringing him back with us."

The dark elf nodded as he pulled a triage bandage from his kit. Enchanted with healing magics, it would stop the bleeding and keep the prince alive at least long enough to get him to actual healers. As he knelt down to the bleeding prince, Kane tried to stop him, trying vainly to protect the injured fairy.

Pullus shoved him aside without even a glance.

Hawk gasped as soon as the bandage touched his neck, the blood stopped gushing, and he passed out instantly. "He was an idiot, but his aim was true," Pullus reported to his leader. "He lives for now." The emphasis on the *now* was not lost on Ater.

Kane watched as Ater took out a piece of chalk and began to draw a circle around himself on the wooden floor. Pullus dragged the prince into the center, giving Kane a warning look: don't try to rescue him.

It was a wasted look.

Kane rushed the two of them, screaming, "Leave him alone!" His fists clenched in rage.

Pullus released the grip of one of his hands on Hawk and backhanded the human almost casually. Kane tried not to call out as he fell back. Pullus dropped Hawk into the circle as Ater finished the circumference. The instant the two lines met, the circle exploded into light, blinding Kane for a moment.

When he opened his eyes, they were gone.

THE chalk had burnt into the rug, like it had been gunpowder that was lit. The smoke was like nothing I'd ever smelt before. "Where did they take him?" I asked Ruber.

"Back to Arcadia," the gem said in my ear.

"What will they do to him?" I asked, not wanting to know the truth.

After a pause, Ruber admitted, "They will torture him for the key to Ascension, most likely maiming or crippling him for life."

I was horrified by the casual way the gem intoned the words. "What if he doesn't talk?" I asked in a panic.

"Everyone talks," Ruber said darkly.

I pushed Ruber's words out of my mind as I said, "Can you get us there?" Ruber paused, which meant yes, but he was hesitant to tell me. If he didn't know, he would have instantly had an excuse why. "Ruber, I order you to open a portal! We have to save Hawk!"

"You couldn't stop one dark elf assassin, what hope do you have against the entirety of the Dark?"

I had no time for logic.

"I don't care! He's in danger, and I need to help him." I hated the way my voice was cracking but didn't care. When he did nothing I screamed, "Ruber! *Now!*"

I heard him sigh as he floated out of my ear and hovered over the charred markings. "Retrieve the pack and place Spike in the circle," he said with obvious disapproval in his voice. "There is no sense in leaving anything behind."

I raced out to the lawn, grabbed the pack, and ran back in as fast as I could. Ruber was tracing the pattern of the runes slowly; the lights beneath him made the ashes begin to pulse with energy. I grabbed Spike's feet and dragged him into the circle. As soon as I had him inside, Ruber made his way around, hovering a few inches from where he had started. I looked down at the carpet, and I saw Hawk's sword lying there, the hilt was stained with blood, which made my blood run cold. I walked over and picked it up determinedly. I could feel the blade pulse in my hand and, for some reason, I found that reassuring.

"I am warning you, Kane, this is a bad idea."

I tried not to scream in anger, instead asking, "They will kill him, won't they?" Ruber said nothing, which was all the answer I needed. I put the sword into the pack and walked back into the circle. "Open the portal, Ruber. Now!"

The lights beneath him flared up again as he completed the circle.

"Kane?" I heard Jewel ask from outside the circle.

I looked up as the ashes burst into flames. I think I heard her scream, but I wasn't sure....

Because I was no longer there, I was no longer anywhere.

JOHN GOODE was found in the back of a garden shed originally, and lured out by candy, he was raised on Elm Street before moving due to a rare sleep disorder. After taking off with a few friends to find a dead body, he attended Sherman High School majoring in absenteeism. Dropping out of college to work at the Gap, he struggled on perfecting his karaoke version of "Conjunction Junction" before moving on. He worked several odd jobs, first as a clerk at a record store that was open till midnight, moving to garbage collector with his brother, and then he finally decided on being a convenience store clerk who complained a lot that he wasn't even supposed to be there that particular day. He lives with a talking cartoon dog or cat or three squirrels and has possibly ingested far too much pop culture over the years.

Or he is this guy who lives in this place and writes stuff he hopes you read. John discovered M/M erotica when he heard himself describing what he had done the previous night.

Also from J<small>OHN</small> G<small>OODE</small>

Harmony Ink

CPSIA information can be obtained at www.ICGtesting.com
Printed in the USA
LVOW120842090312

272330LV00001B/20/P